TAKING HER VIKINGS

ACADEMY OF TIME BOOK 1

SKYE MACKINNON

Peryton Press

CONTENTS

AUTHOR'S NOTE

Dear Readers,

Ever since I started publishing, I wanted to write about Vikings, but I lacked the confidence to do so. I wanted it to be accurate, as close to the historical facts as possible, and didn't think I had the knowledge and resources to do so.

Last year, I started a Master's Degree that involved taking a course in Runology and Old Norse. I find the language absolutely fascinating, and even though the grammar is quite complex, the vocabulary isn't. There's a surprising amount of words in Old Norse that are similar to modern English, French and German words, which helps a lot when trying to understand a saga or an old runestone.

After a semester of studying runes and Viking records, I finally felt ready to at least start writing a book about Norse culture. One thing that really helped was realising that we don't know as much about Vikings as I thought we did. Take the pronunciation. There are no auditory records of how Old Norse was spoken, and while we can look at how today's Icelandic and Scandinavian languages are articulated, we have no guarantee that it's the same as the Vikings would have pronounced it.

In addition to that, most of what we know comes from archaeological evidence and from written records, including the famous sagas, gravestones and rune carvings. Those written stories are mostly about famous people though. They don't give us all the details of daily life, and there's always the doubt that the author may have overexaggerated some things for dramatic effect.

Basically, I realised I shouldn't have been as scared to venture into writing about Vikings. I'm going to try and stick close to what we know about their lives, but I'm also accepting that this is fiction. There will be deviations from how it may actually have been back then. I may make mistakes in portraying my Vikings. But that's okay. I'm here to tell a story, and just like the saga writers, I may overexaggerate occasionally. Call it creative freedom.

Saying that, I've tried my best to make sure that all the Old Norse vocabulary is correct (no, my Viking Studies professor will never know why I asked her for checking some expressions and spellings).

If you're interested in learning more about Viking runes and Old Norse, keep reading after the final chapter to find some resources that may be helpful.

By the way, you can also listen to this book as audiobook!

Enjoy *Taking Her Vikings*!
Skye MacKinnon

Jafnan er hálfsögð saga ef einn segir.
A tale is but half told when only one person tells it.

The Saga of Grettir, chapter 46

Ground Floor

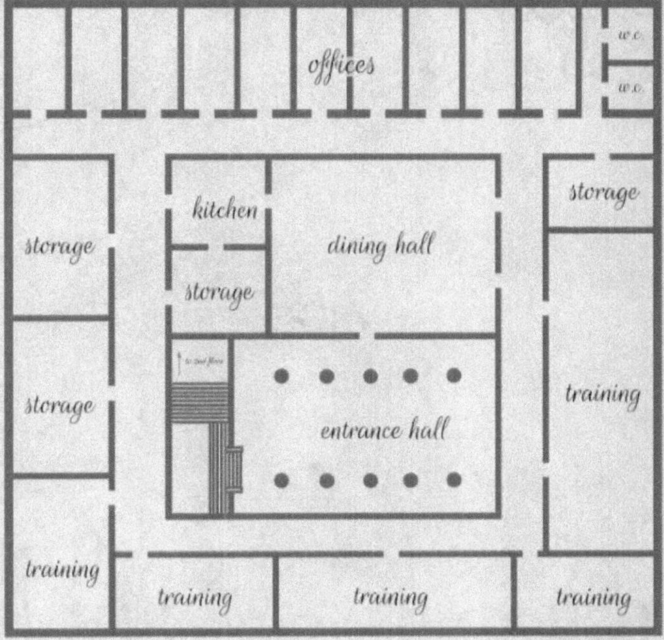

I looked at my mother one last time, then turned away. I'd prepared for this moment for weeks, but it had still come as a shock. For both of us. There were streaks of tears on both our cheeks and if I turned around, I'd see her tears drop onto her pretty red blouse. But no. I wasn't going to look at her again. If I did, I'd run back and stay.

"Ready?" the woman next to me asked. She'd never given me her name, but it was obvious that she was employed by the Academy. Only TTA staff wore the white and blue uniform with a starched white collar, a row of silver ear studs and a set of cyber bracelets.

I clenched my fists, fighting the impulse to return to my mother. It was the price of acceptance. Never see your family again. By going to the Academy, I was making sure that my mother would be provided for until the day she died, but it wasn't an easy price to pay. We'd always been close, especially after dad left. It had taken her months to convince me to apply to TTA. Eventually, I'd given in, never actually believing that I'd be accepted. It was a one in a million, hell, one in a billion chance.

"Ready," I replied. A shiver ran down my back. This was it. The moment everything was going to change.

"Take my hands and whatever happens, don't let go. I don't want to lose you before you even arrive at the Academy."

The woman's voice wasn't unkind, but it held a certain dispassion that told me that the only reason she cared about my wellbeing was a professional one. They'd probably sack her if she killed a student in transit.

Her hands were freezing, making me realise how cold the day had become. It smelled like snow. Was it going to be snowing at the Academy? Nobody knew where it was located. It could have been in the centre of the Sahara Desert, for all I knew.

The woman gripped my hands tight and began to count. "Three.... two... one..."

Sunshine burst from the skies, drenching us in beams of light. Seconds later, we were in the air, racing through time and space, our bodies nothing but flecks of light. That's how I imagined it, anyway, after being taught about the mysteries of porting at school. It was something only the rich could afford, so the teachers basically told us to not get our hopes up of ever actually experiencing it. I doubted any of them had experience of porting themselves; otherwise, they wouldn't have become teachers in our shitty inner-city school.

It only took a couple of seconds before we reached our destination, but I wished it would have lasted an eternity. I'd never felt so light, so carefree. There was so much space around us, sparkling with opportunities and hope. Life had always been claustrophobic in our tiny flat on the third floor of a massive tower block. Knowing there were hundreds of people living above us made me feel small and besieged. Insignificant. This, however, was the exact opposite. Even though the light and shadows around us didn't make any sense, didn't conform to my usual perception of reality, it all felt *big*.

Our landing was abrupt and painful. Gravity and sound crashed into me, making me stumble and fall onto the hard ground.

"Buckets are to your right," the woman said and walked away, the heels of her shoes making little echoey sounds as she walked. We seemed to be in a stone building, but my eyes weren't ready to function yet. Lights flashed across my vision, followed by white fog. I blinked several times, trying to restore my sight.

Had she mentioned buckets? Why would I need a bucket?

A retching sound from my left told me exactly why. The smell of puke followed the sound a moment later, and I held my hands over my mouth and nose. Yuck. Someone stumbled past me towards the buckets, almost tripping over my legs. More heaving and groaning. Whoever was making these noises really wasn't feeling well.

Something wet touched my lips. Was I crying? I lifted my hands to my eyes, but they were dry. I licked my lips. The iron taste of blood surprised me. I touched my nose. It was bleeding. Damn. Luckily, I had a couple of used tissues in my coat pockets, so I scrunched one of them and stuck parts of it into my nostrils to stem the bleeding. Hopefully, it would stop soon.

Slowly, my vision returned, although everything still looked a little foggy. I was in a large hall, surrounded by other people kneeling on the ground. Now that I had a closer look, I realised that the stone floor was actually marble. Posh. Wide marble columns reached up to the ceiling which was so high that I couldn't really make it out with my impaired eyesight. Behind the two columns in front of me, a staircase led up to a pair of old wooden doors. This room had to be at least as big as my entire school had been, and there wasn't even furniture in here. Just empty space with a couple of plastic buckets stacked up in a corner. After growing up in a city where space was at a premium, this felt like a bit of a waste.

The retcher slowly stumbled back to wherever they'd come from, but the smell didn't disappear. I got to my feet and walked towards the staircase. If I didn't get away from that smell, I'd have to throw up myself.

Just when I reached the bottom step, the large doors opened with a low rumble. There was a bright light on the other side, so bright that the man's shape was visible only as a silhouette. I blinked, but my eyes weren't able yet to make out the details. All I could see was that it was a large man in a white form-fitting suit, probably the Academy's uniform.

"Attention!" he called out with a booming voice. "Everyone who threw up, assemble to my right. Everyone who didn't, stand at my left."

Groans followed his words. Several people didn't sound like they were ready to stand yet. I walked to his left, then realised that I was still having a used tissue hanging from my nostrils. I removed it as quickly as I could without anyone else seeing it. No idea why it embarrassed me; it was better than throwing up into a plastic bucket.

It took forever for everyone to assemble. Only two

others were joining me on the left, both of them girls. They seemed younger than me, but I was old to join TTA. Most people joined up straight after leaving school, but that was when my mother had fallen ill and I had much more important things to think of back then. Like whether she would survive. Now, two years later, she was back to full health, but our savings were non-existent and our debts towering above us like nightmare creatures. I'd applied for dozens of jobs, but with a two-year gap on my CV, I'd had nothing but rejections. Until the letter from TTA arrived.

"Looks like it's only us," one of the girls muttered. She had striking red hair with yellow ends, making it look like flames were flickering around her head. She was taller than me and thin as a beanstalk. Her chest was flat and I suddenly felt a little self-conscious about my boobs that barely fit into my bra.

"Did all of them puke?" I asked bewildered, staring at the group of at least thirty people on the other side of the hall. "It wasn't that bad."

The girl grinned. "Maybe they're just not cut out to be here. I've heard that they're weeding out people in the first few weeks to make sure only those talented enough stay. Maybe the three of us will be the only ones to stay."

"Or maybe we're the ones who failed," the other girl whispered ominously. She was an entire head shorter than me. Her hair was covered in a purple headscarf and her wide black dress hid most of her shape. She was wearing black gloves and somehow, I didn't think it was because of the cold.

A pit opened in my stomach. What if she was right? If I was expelled from TTA before I'd even had my first paycheck, I'd not be able to provide for my mum. I'd be back at square zero.

"Welcome to the Academy," the man said with his beautiful deep voice. I was sure he'd be a great singer. He turned to the pukers and smiled. "Well done for making it here in one piece. We only lost one today, which I think is a new record. Don't see being nauseous as a weakness. It's normal for most to experience some discomfort when porting."

The pit in my stomach grew. If this was normal, then the three of us were decidedly unnormal. Did my nose-bleed count as the same? Should I be standing on the other side?

The man turned to us. "The three of you didn't throw up?"

I shook my head.

"Did the porting affect you in some other way?" he asked.

Fire-hair girl cleared her throat. "I've got a headache and my vision is kind of fuzzy."

The girl in the headscarf didn't say anything, so I guessed it was my turn. "I had a nosebleed and the same foggy vision. It's almost back to normal now though." I added the last bit hurriedly, almost like an apology. I still didn't know what all this was about.

"My stomach hurts," the third girl said quietly. "I can see alright though."

The man nodded and smiled. "All of those symptoms are normal." He spread his arms and pointed towards two doors at opposite ends of the hall. "You'll be housed in different wings of the Academy. The three of you who didn't exhibit signs of nausea will be in the fast-track class, since you have the potential to travel the furthest back in time. The rest of you will be in the standard class, proceeding with the regular curriculum."

Murmurs came from the pukers. I could almost feel their jealous stares. To be honest, I would have preferred to swap places. Fast-track class? I didn't know anything about time travel, I was a complete newbie. I wanted to take it slow, learn everything I could. If I failed because I travelled too soon, I'd be expelled. Or I'd be stuck in history, trapped forever. I clenched my fists. I couldn't fail. I'd not leave my mother starving. I was going to succeed, even if that meant I'd have to stay up every night to study.

"This is great," fire-hair girl grinned. "We're special. We might be able to travel within weeks! Imagine, going back in time. I've always wanted to meet a hot stone age guy."

"Socrates," the girl in the headscarf muttered dreamily. "Hippocrates. Pythagoras. Plato. Do you think we get to choose to when we travel?"

"No idea," I replied. "I don't think anyone knows. It's not like the Academy advertises the details of what they do."

"My uncle is a TA," fire-hair girl said with a smirk. "He's told me stuff. Top secret. I bet I'm going to be top of the class with that knowledge."

I couldn't help but roll my eyes. She could be top of the class for all I cared. I wanted to know what to do, how to travel, I didn't care about grades. I never had. Grades were just numbers, they didn't mean anything. What mattered was what was stored in my head.

Headscarf girl met my eyes and smiled. "I'm Maryam," she said and held out a gloved hand.

"Lainie."

We shook hands. Her grip was strong, surprising me.

"Where are you from?" I asked. The Academy took people from all over the world, as long as they spoke sufficient English to follow the classes. That made me wonder, were there other academies for other languages?

"Lyon in France, but I was born in Sudan," she said. "You?"

"New London."

"I'm Kaycee from Chicago," fire-hair girl interrupted before I could say more. "Have you ever been to the States?"

Both of us shook our heads.

"I bet the Academy is somewhere in the US," Kaycee said with a proud grin. "All the important things are."

Maryam rolled her eyes. "Have you looked at the architecture? This building is far too old to be in the States. I'm betting Europe, maybe somewhere in Germany or Austria judging from the style of the columns. See those carvings at the top of the door? Definitely European."

Before Kaycee could reply, a young woman joined our group. She was wearing the Academy's uniform. I realised that she had only two silver studs in her left earlobe. The woman who'd brought me here had five on one side and four on the other. Were they an indication of rank?

"I'm Sue, your assigned mentor," she said with a cheery smile. Her blue eyes twinkled as she took us in. "I'm going to show you around, assign your quarters, and if you have any questions, I'm the one you should come to. I won't be doing any of the teaching, but outside of lessons, I'm your main contact. Any problems, I'll be there to solve them."

Her smile was genuine; she really meant it. I smiled back at her. It was good to have someone around who was both friendly and knowledgeable. I was going to follow her around like a puppy until I knew the ropes. I wasn't the most confident of people, not in new situations anyway. If it was necessary, I could take charge and step over my own shadow, but for now, I was going to soak in as much knowledge as I could.

"We have both single rooms and dormitories," she continued. "Which would you prefer?"

"Single," I said quickly at the same time as Kaycee.

"I'm fine with a dormitory," Maryam muttered. "I'm used to sleeping in one room with my sister."

I shot her a pitying look. I was lucky in that I was only leaving behind my mother. Other people had entire families and large groups of friends that they'd never see again. Most of my friends had moved away after we graduated from high school, which meant that I didn't really have anyone who'd miss me besides my mum.

Sue grinned. "That means that you two will share a room and you," she pointed at Maryam, "will get a single room. We like to put people out of their comfort zones here. You won't always get what you want."

I sighed. I should have stayed quiet or pretended that I liked being around people at all times.

"Is there no way to upgrade?" Kaycee asked in a whiny voice. "My uncle went to TTA as well."

Sue shrugged. "We don't care about your family or your connections. Everyone starts at the same level here. Now let's go before we miss dinner."

CHAPTER 2

S ue didn't give us any time to properly look around our new home. Luckily, the room I was to share with Kaycee was bigger than the one I'd had for myself back at my mum's place. Our beds were on opposite ends of the room and a tall bookshelf acted as a screen for privacy. Two large wardrobes were close to the door. None of us had brought any clothes - we weren't allowed to take anything with us to TTA - so that meant they would either stay very empty or the Academy would provide us with enough things to fill them with.

There was nothing else in the room. No decoration, not even windows. I still didn't know where the Academy was located. All the walls were bare stone, no wallpaper or paint anywhere. It was kind of pretty and atmospheric, but also a little depressing. It didn't feel like a home, not like a place I was going to be comfortable in for the next few years. Not that I had a clue of how long our training would be. When signing up for TTA training, it's a commitment for life. All you know is that your family will be looked after and that you'll never want for anything.

That's enough to make most people want to join. The world can be a hard place and TTA offers security that is hard to find in other professions.

"Hurry up, dinner's getting cold," Sue scolded, waiting outside the door with Maryam. "It's first come, first serve in the dining hall and you don't want to be last, trust me."

I gave my new room one last glance, then quickly followed our guide. She led us along a corridor that seemed to house more bedrooms like ours, and into a small common room. Plastic chairs were dotted around the area, all of them empty. Everyone else had to be at dinner. A couple of bookshelves lined the walls, one of them topped with a stack of board games. That was it. No television, no computers, not even a fireplace or radiators. TTA surely liked sparse interior design. I would miss my mum's soft sofa with its dozens of cushions and blankets. These plastic chairs looked decidedly uncomfortable.

"Whenever you're not in lessons, training or studying, you can spend time in the common room," Sue explained hurriedly. "Books have to stay in here. No taking them into bedrooms. You only go into your room to sleep."

"Why?" Kaycee interrupted. "What if we want some privacy?"

Sue laughed, not unkindly. "As a level one student, you don't have privacy. It's something you have to earn. Work hard, complete all your assignments as best as you can, and you'll slowly earn more privileges. The faster you learn, the more benefits you'll get."

Kaycee crossed her arms in front of her chest, obviously not pleased with that reply. She'd probably expected to get special treatment because of her uncle.

"The bathrooms are at the other end of the corridor we just came from. I'm sure you know how to use a shower?" Sue laughed. "Good, then let's get some food. I'm starving."

Compared to the other parts of the Academy, the dining hall had a completely different atmosphere. The sound of hundreds of people eating and chatting filled the air, together with the smell of a wild variety of dishes. There were painting and tapestries all over the stone walls, and the high ceiling was covered in what looked like fairy lights. It gave it a homely, friendly feel. For the first time, I thought that I might be able to make this my home.

Sue led us to a buffet at the very end of the hall.

"Choose whatever you want, but don't expect there to be enough left for second helpings," she said with a grin. "The good stuff disappears fast when you have two hundred students, teachers and agents all starving. You'll see soon that you're going to eat more here than you're used to. A side effect of your training."

"Do we have assigned seats?" Maryam asked and I followed her gaze, taking in the square tables filling the hall, each of them with four chairs. They were wooden chairs, looking much more comfortable than the plastic ones in our common room.

"No, sit wherever you like. Once you get to know people, I'm sure the usual cliques will form. It's part of Academy life." Sue snickered. "Will you find the way back to the common room after dinner?"

I nodded.

"Good. I'll see if I can procure some maps of the building. I know there are some, but I couldn't find any earlier today. That will make it easier for you to find your classrooms tomorrow."

Excitement bubbled up in me. Lessons. I'd learn how to be a time agent. Travel through time, meet people from the past, and save the present in the process. Not that I had any idea of how exactly that was done. But everyone knew that the TTA was responsible for helping us out of the last recession, and cure at least two major diseases. Somehow, they used the past to improve the present.

Kaycee pushed past me and rushed towards the vegetarian part of the buffet. Maryam followed her, but I was drawn towards the scent of curry and spices. It was a table at the very end of the long row, and most of the bowls and platters were still full. Three large pots of curry, a covered plate of naan bread, a basket filled with poppadoms and, were those pakora? Oh my goodness, I was in heaven. I'd always loved Indian food and now, I could eat as much as I wanted. I took a plate from a stack and heaved as much food on it as it could carry. I certainly wasn't going to starve at the Academy.

I looked around for a place to sit. Most tables were full or only had one empty place, so it was clear that I wasn't going to be able to sit with Maryam and Kaycee. Sue had disappeared, probably sitting with her friends and colleagues. I hadn't figured out yet if she was a senior student or a member of the Academy staff.

The closest table was occupied by only one man. His broad back was turned towards me. It seemed as good a place as any to sit. If I wanted to be part of TTA, I would have to get to know people.

"Is it okay if I join you?" I asked, carefully balancing my overfull plate. It was getting hot at the edges.

"Go ahead," the man said in a deep voice that carried a slight accent. "That's what chairs are for. To sit on."

I frowned at his strange manner but sat down and took some cutlery from a holder in the centre of the table.

I ate several mouthfuls before realising that I hadn't introduced myself or even properly looked at the man. I wasn't usually this impolite, but porting and all the excitement of being in a new place had made me hungry.

He was staring at me. Not in a friendly, interested way, but in an intense and scrutinising way that made a shiver run down my back.

"You're hungry," he observed, his gaze never leaving my face. Since he obviously didn't see anything wrong with staring at me like a zoo animal, I returned the favour. He was older than me, maybe in his early thirties. His eyes were the colour of azure waters, the kind of tropical water that I'd only seen on television. They were guarded by thick eyebrows, just as blond as his hair and beard. The beard was well-trimmed with not a single hair out of place; it was obvious that he took great care of keeping it that way. His hair was close to shoulder-length and a lot messier than his beard. Like he hadn't combed it in days.

"Like what you see?"

His lips curved into a taunting smile. Not unfriendly, just mocking.

"I'm not sure yet," I replied with a blank expression. I was good at those. Keeping others in the dark about what I was feeling. "Are you one of the teachers?"

He nodded. "And you're a newbie. Only newbies sit on my table. By tomorrow, you'll be somewhere else."

"Why?"

"Because by then, you'll know who I am," he said

mysteriously. "But for now, I'm going to enjoy your company. What's your name?"

What a strange man. His plate was empty, so he didn't have to stay here. The dining hall was slowly getting quieter as more and more people left. It seemed he really wanted to have a conversation.

"Lainie. What's yours?"

"Hjalmar. Most people can't pronounce it properly."

"Hjalmar," I repeated, trying to make it sound as rough as he'd said it, although I couldn't copy his accent. "Is that a Scandinavian name?"

"It's an ancient word," he replied, staring at me intently. "Do you speak any foreign languages?"

I frowned at his abrupt change of topic. "Some French, but it's a couple of years ago since I last spoke any. I've probably forgotten most of it." I took a bite of naan bread, but made sure to keep my eyes fixed on him. He was playing some kind of game, and I sure was going to match him. I was competitive like that.

"Your pronunciation was excellent. Were you good at your French lessons?"

I shrugged. "Not top of the class but I found it quite easy to learn the language. I never had to read over new vocabulary more than once or twice before I could remember the words."

"Good. That will help you in my class."

"Your class?" I couldn't help but sound surprised. I'd known he was a teacher, but I hadn't really expected him to be mine. He didn't seem like the kind of teacher you had at the very beginning of your training. Not with the intense way he was looking at me, like he could see into my mind.

"Have you not checked your timetable yet?"

I shook my head. "I haven't been given one."

He chuckled. "Tomorrow at ten in the morning. Although by then, you'll probably have heard the rumours, now that people have seen you sit at my table. Don't let that influence you from learning as much as you can in my class."

His eyes had turned a little sad. It sounded like people usually avoided him. It couldn't just be because of his strange manner. Well, if he was right, I was going to find out soon.

I turned around and looked at the people at the neighbouring tables. Some of them were openly staring at me. Or at Hjalmar, it was hard to tell. Had I managed to get myself a reputation just by sitting at his table? What a way to start.

"Ten a.m. Don't be late."

He got up, his chair screeching over the stone floor. He left without another glance, but dozens of stares followed him.

CHAPTER 3

Morning came far too soon. A loud bell echoed through the room, followed by groans from Kaycee. I yawned and pulled my duvet over my head. She'd snored all night and I hadn't got nearly as much sleep as I wanted. Or needed.

"What time is it?" I asked no one in particular. I hadn't brought a watch with me, and there wasn't a clock in the room. Without the terrible bell, we would have slept in.

"Feels like midnight," Kaycee grumbled. "Do you think they let us sleep in at weekends?"

I sighed. "There's training at weekends. Didn't you look at your timetable?"

When we'd returned to our room last night, both a map and a timetable had been waiting for us on our beds, together with silky pyjamas and a set of toiletries. The wardrobes had also been stocked with white TTA uniforms as well as some casual clothes.

No idea how they'd got our sizes right. Or had we given them our clothes size on the application form? I couldn't remember, it had been months ago that I applied for TTA. Being here still felt like a bit of a dream.

The bell rang for a second time. I wanted to cuddle up under my blanket, ignoring the early morning, but this was my first day and I didn't want to start it by being late.

With a deep sigh, I threw back my duvet and climbed out of bed. Kaycee's only reaction was to push her pillow onto her head. I smiled. Guess we both weren't morning people. At least one thing we had in common.

I opened my wardrobe and took in what was on offer. Were we expected to wear the white uniform? Or was that just for assignments? I wished they'd given us some more information on what we were supposed to do. It was all a bit confusing and I didn't want to make a mistake right at the start. There were rumours that it was easy to get expelled from the Academy, and that was one thing I couldn't afford to happen.

I decided to play it safe and put on a uniform. The white fabric clung to my skin, exposing every curve that I would have liked to hide. The collar rubbed uncomfortably against my neck, but hopefully, that would get better after wearing it for a while.

"You better get up," I warned Kaycee as the bell chimed for the third time. "I bet it will be the same thing with breakfast as it is with dinner. First come, first serve."

That made her look up from behind her pillow.

"Do you think there'll be pancakes?"

I shrugged. "Who knows, but there's only one way to find out."

Kaycee sighed and sat up. Her fiery hair was flat against her head, perfectly straight as if she'd never slept on it at all. No, I wasn't jealous. Not at all.

I looked at my timetable again while Kaycee got

ready. The first lesson started at nine, then hourly lessons until noon. One hour for lunch, then all afternoon was reserved for training. Whatever that meant. After dinner, there were two hours of shared revision, then two more hours common room time. I hoped they would let us go to bed before those two hours were up. I couldn't imagine staying in that bland, dull room for that long.

"Let's go," Kaycee said, flinging her hair back in one smooth motion. "I don't want to be late."

I rolled my eyes but followed her without comment.

The dining hall was full of tired looking students. This time, there were almost no teachers and agents. Were they allowed to sleep for longer? I certainly hoped so, that would give me something to look forward to.

I sleepwalked to the buffet and filled a bowl with cornflakes and milk. There was a big selection of hot food, but I didn't like to eat too much in the morning. My stomach felt like it was still asleep.

This time, I found an empty table. A large pot of tea and one that looked like coffee were in the centre of the table, along with a stack of mugs. I poured myself some tea. There was no milk, but I was too tired to stand up and get some from the buffet.

I hated mornings.

Two girls joined me along with Maryam. She looked completely awake, smiling at me with a sparkle in her eyes.

"Good morning, she said with a wide grin. "Are you ready for the first lesson?"

I nodded, focusing on my cornflakes.

"Not a morning person?"

I shook my head and she chuckled. "My dad always said, you simply have to imagine that it isn't morning, but the middle of the day. That drives the tiredness away."

I looked at her sceptically. "I don't think that's going to work."

Maryam shrugged. "I don't think so either, but it's what he said." She turned to the black-haired girl on her right. "Have you met Stacey yet? She's new too."

I introduced myself and Stacey gave me a small smile. She seemed shy, unwilling to meet anyone's eyes.

"You talked to Hjalmar last night," the other girl said without telling us her name. She had beautiful amber eyes surrounded by dark lashes, but the scowl on her face made her seem less pretty.

"Yes, I did," I said calmly. After dinner, I'd gone straight to bed, so I'd not heard any of the rumours the teacher had warned me about. Now, I was curious but also a little apprehensive. I didn't like gossip and knew it was taken with not just a pinch, but an entire spoonful of salt.

"What did he say?" the girl asked, greed shining in her eyes.

I took my time swallowing a spoonful of cornflakes before I replied. "Nothing special. Just that he was a teacher. Why? What's so special about him?"

The girl stared at me. "You don't know?"

"Even I've already heard about him," Stacey muttered. "One of the girls in my dormitory warned me about him."

"Warned?" I asked, suddenly a little worried. "Why?"

The other girl grinned as if she was looking forward to my reaction. I made sure my expression was blank, unwilling to give her the satisfaction.

"He killed a student," she whispered dramatically. "He took him into the past and killed him there."

"Killed him?" Maryam gasped. "Why would he do that?"

"And how would anyone know?" I asked. "Did anyone see it? I thought time agents travelled solo."

Amber-eyes snickered. "When he returned, he was covered in blood. He was suspended for a year, but now he's back. I have no idea why the headmistress would allow him to teach, but luckily, he's restricted to teaching newbies." She grinned at me. "Beware, he's unpredictable. If I were you, I'd avoid him like the murderer he is."

With that, she got up, dramatically stalking away, her hips swaying.

"Weird," Maryam exhaled. "I doubt they'd let a murderer teach us."

"She didn't tell you everything," Stacey whispered. "Julie said that he'd brought back the student's severed hand."

I exchanged a dubious glance with Maryam. It was good to see that I wasn't the only one not instantly believing this gossip.

"We have a lesson with him at ten," I said, feeling a little defiant. "Maybe he'll mention it then."

Stacey's eyes widened and she quickly pulled out her timetable from her bag. She sighed in relief. "I don't have him as a teacher. Seems he only does the fast-track class."

A loud gong interrupted our conversation. It was a nicer bell than the alarm ring this morning, but it made my stomach go a little queasy. Now, Academy life was going to start for real.

INSTEAD OF THE history lesson we were supposed to have, the headmistress awaited us in our classroom together with four other teachers in the Academy uniform. I was glad now that I had put it on this morning. About a quarter of students were wearing casual clothes, making them stand out in the sea of white. To be honest, a white uniform didn't seem very practical. I hoped we wouldn't have to do our own laundry. It would be a never-ending stain fight.

"I'm Professor Tape," the headmistress introduced herself. I'd seen her at dinner last night when one of the other students had pointed her out, but this was the first time I'd heard her speak. Her voice was melodic, almost musical, somehow reminding me of the man who'd welcomed us the night before. Maybe they were related? Or was it part of the job of running TTA to have a pretty voice?

Professor Tape was an older Asian woman in her sixties, her grey hair sprinkled with white highlights. Her face was smooth except for a few soft wrinkles around her eyes. She was the only teacher not in a white uniform. Hers was black as the night, the only colour some golden stitching around the collar and the sleeves. It was a contrast that immediately made her stand out.

She was small, the smallest of the five people at the front of the classroom, but that didn't diminish her air of authority. She waited until everyone had taken a seat - except for a few stragglers who had to stand at the back because this classroom really wasn't made for this many people - then turned around and scribbled on the blackboard. It was old-fashioned for a school that was all about teaching us the technology needed to travel in time. We'd had nothing but digital whiteboards back at my high school, and even those were a little out of date.

"T. T. A.," she said as she wrote the letters on the board. "Time Travel Academy. The only school in the world where you can travel into the past as part of your studies."

She turned to us and smiled. "And you've all made it here. Lovely. Welcome to the Academy. Being selected means that you're some of the brightest and most talented young people. Thousands apply to us each year, and we only take thirty at the most. This year, we have twenty-eight."

I quickly looked around the room. I'd soon get to know everyone here. These were going to be the people I'd spend all my time with. Living at a school was strange. Back when I was in high school, there was a clear separation between school and personal life. Here, it was all muddled up. As Sue had said, there wasn't going to be any privacy. Twenty-four hours surrounded by the same people. For an introvert like me, this wasn't going to be easy. I'd spent the last two years with my mother, rarely seeing other people besides shopkeepers, doctors and the occasional friend of my mum's. I'd got used to being on my own.

"Three of you managed to be admitted to the fast-track programme," Professor Tape continued. "Raise your hands, please."

Kaycee immediately waved her arm, desperate for attention. I resisted the urge to roll my eyes and lifted my own hand.

"The three of you will share some of your classes with

the rest of the Hummingbirds, but you'll also have some more intense tuition to prepare you for your first jumps through time."

"Hummingbirds, Professor?" A boy at the back asked.

"Has nobody explained this yet? First-year students are called Hummingbirds, then you become Nightingales, then Seagulls and finally Eagles. Four years of study await you. By the end, maybe ten of you will remain." Her voice turned serious. "This Academy values talent, but we don't tolerate bad and irresponsible behaviour. If you misbehave or fail at your studies, you will be expelled, no matter how talented you are." She turned to our small trio of fast-trackers. "That goes for the three of you, too."

One of the four teachers took a stack of papers from the desk and began to hand them out.

Rules of the Time Travel Academy.

1. You may not leave the Academy premises without permission.
2. Everything that happens at the Academy is confidential. You may not talk about TTA business to outsiders.
3. No contact with family members until you graduate from the Academy. This includes electronic communication.
4. We operate a strict hierarchy. Students in higher years have authority over students in lower years. Teachers have the absolute authority, only superseded by the headteacher and official time agents.
5. Graduating from the Academy does not guarantee a job as a time agent.

6. Time travel is dangerous. We take no responsibility for injuries or fatalities resulting from reckless behaviour.
7. No unsupervised time travel. No use of equipment without a teacher present.
8. For additional rules, please refer to the Time Travel Regulations and the Student Behaviour Manual.

I SWALLOWED HARD. The truth of it all was beginning to sink in. This was real. This was happening. I smiled. I was ready for it.

"Over the next few years, you will study a variety of subjects," Professor Tape continued once she'd made sure that we'd all read the rules. "While the Hummingbird is very generic and targeted to prepare you for time travel in general, the following years focus very much on the time periods you will be visiting. At the end of this year, you will undergo a series of tests that will determine how far back in the past you will be allowed to travel. This decision will be final. If you're caught travelling further back than what your certification allows, you will be expelled from the Academy. In your second year, you will study mostly history and foreign languages to prepare for your first assignments. To become a Seagull, you will have to successfully undergo your first unsupervised time travel."

My heart began to beat faster at the prospect. This couldn't come soon enough. I wanted to learn all about it, how to travel, how to integrate with past cultures, how it would all help our present society.

"In your third year, you will study psychology, the art

of seduction and a range of techniques that will help you survive in the past."

"Art of seduction?" Kaycee whispered behind me. "I don't need to learn that. I've been pulling guys since I grew boobs."

I suppressed a snicker.

"Your Eagle year will be mostly self-study," the head-mistress continued. "You will work on your own independent projects and will be assigned a tutor each who will guide and advise you. Depending on how well you perform throughout that final year, you will be offered a position as a time agent, as staff here at TTA or another job."

Another job? What was that going to be? The Academy was all about preparing us for time travel. I doubted I would be able to be happy with a mundane office job after four years of study. I steeled my jaw. I was going to succeed. I was going to put everything I had into my studies. Time travel couldn't be all that hard, could it?

By the end of the introductory session, my confidence had crumbled away. We'd been given even more rules, even more warnings, and several stories of how students had been expelled for minor mistakes. I knew they were trying to scare us into behaving well, but their tactic was working. The knot in my stomach was growing. It felt like they were heaping pressure on us, more and more until only some of us were able to withstand it. Weeding out the people cut out for this job. I had thought getting into the Academy was hard. Now it turned out that staying here was going to be a whole lot harder.

Being in a large classroom all by ourselves was strange. Maryam and Kaycee were sitting on either side of me, in the second row, which seemed better than sitting right at the front. Hjalmar was running late. Was I even going to be able to call him that? Or did we have to call him Mister something? Professor Murderer?

I glanced at my TTA branded notebook. We'd each been given a bag full of stationary at the end of the intro session, and told that we could get more supplies at the student support office. Not that I knew where that was yet. We had a map, but no time to actually explore. I took it out and studied it for the tenth time. The building was four floors tall, with the top floor reserved for teachers and staff. The ground floor had the dining hall, a big kitchen, some unspecified offices as well as rooms labelled 'training'. On the first floor were our dorms and bedroom, the common rooms, bathrooms and a couple of storage rooms. The second floor was where we were now. Classrooms, labs, a lecture theatre, and the library.

Something was bothering me about the map, but I couldn't figure out what it was. I ran a finger over the entrance hall where we'd arrived yesterday. It was adjacent to the dining hall and surrounded by several training rooms, plus the staircase leading to the first floor. Just a normal room. Nothing special, except for its size.

"Something wrong?"

Hjalmar's voice made me sit up straight. I'd not noticed him enter the room, let alone see him approach our table.

I shook my head. "Just getting familiar with the map."

He stared at me, his lips twitching. "Noticed something strange?"

I looked up at him in surprise and his smirk widened into a grin. "I'm not sure," I muttered, annoyed that I hadn't figured it out yet. "But something is off."

Hjalmar nodded. "Indeed. Let me know when you realise the truth. Most people get a little anxious when they do."

"What are you talking about?" Kaycee demanded. "It's just a map."

The teacher turned to her and looked at fire-hair girl from top to bottom. "Yes, it's just a map."

He stepped back and sat down on his desk, his legs casually spread. My eyes were almost automatically drawn to his crotch, before I quickly looked back up, taking in the rest of him. In contrast to the teachers earlier, he wasn't wearing the white TTA uniform. He was in tight black leather trousers and a red plaid shirt that was unbuttoned one button too far down to be professional. Some blond chest hair was peeking through, making me wonder what the rest of his chest looked like.

From the way his shirt was stretched in places, I imagined him to be muscular beneath his clothes. Hard, defined muscles.

No, I had to stop thinking like that. He was my teacher. We were all adults here, but there was a distinct line between students and teachers that shouldn't be crossed. No matter how good-looking the teacher was. No matter how much his smirk provoked me. He knew exactly what I was thinking, and he enjoyed teasing me. His eyes were locked with mine, completely ignoring that there were two other people in the room. The longer I looked into his eyes, the brighter their beautiful blue shimmer seemed. I could get lost in those eyes...

Maryam cleared her throat and the spell was broken. My cheeks heated when I realised that I had blatantly been checking out my teacher. I now wished I'd sat somewhere else at dinner last night. This wasn't going to end well. I had to stay away from him before I turned into a lovesick teenager with a crush on a sexy teacher.

"I'm here to teach you the way of the Vikings," Hjalmar said, pointing at a poster near the door. It was covered in runes. "That includes Old Norse and the Futhark."

Kaycee raised her hand. "Why do we need to speak their language? Don't we get one of those translator implants that does it for you?"

Hjalmar frowned at her. "What happens if the implant breaks? What will you do when you're stranded in the past, unable to communicate with the people you're staying with? They will turn against you, they'll see you as an enemy, or an evil spirit if you're particularly unlucky. Besides, a language teaches you a lot about a culture. In Old Norse, the word for sword is sverð, but if you were feeling poetic, you could also call it a war-leek or a wound-hoe."

He turned to the blackboard and wrote down several words that looked like gibberish to me.

sterkr bani hvess viðar — the strong killer of every tree

bǫl markar — the harm of the forest

húsþjófr — the house-thief

aldrnari — life-nourisher

"All these phrases can be expressed in a single word. Can anyone guess what it is?"

I read through the list several times, but before I could tell Hjalmar my answer, Kaycee let out a dramatic sigh. "Does that mean we don't just have to learn the normal words, but also these poetic expressions?"

The teacher grinned. "Yes, and the runes to spell them, obviously. You're not going to start speaking Old Norse overnight. You do, however, have the advantage that I may be able to take you on field trips to let you hear the language being spoken by other native speakers."

"Other?" I blurted before I could stop myself.

He ignored me, which only made my mind spin faster. Old Norse wasn't spoken nowadays, it hadn't been for centuries. That meant... my teacher was a Viking. Fuck me.

"An axe?" Maryam suggested, reminding me of the riddle.

"Fire," I said quickly, before going back to opening my mind to the prospect of having a real-life Viking in the room with me. And we hadn't even travelled in time.

"Can't we just call it fire?" Kaycee moaned, oblivious to the big revelation. "I don't get why we need to make it so complicated."

Hjalmar frowned at her. "You can call it fire, but what

if a Norseman talks to you about the sacred life-nourisher and you don't know what he means? It could get you in trouble, and trouble is what you want to avoid during time travel."

Maryam lifted her hand. "Were all those fire expressions used during the same period or did they develop over time? I'm just thinking, what if we call it the house-thief and they don't actually use that expression yet? What if they then add it to their vocabulary? Wouldn't that be bad? Create a paradox?"

Hjalmar gave her a smile. "Very good. That's why we stick to using basic vocabulary ourselves and leave the flowery phrases to the natives. The main thing is that you understand them. But before you can learn Old Norse, you need to know the Futhark."

He got up from the desk and walked to the poster he'd pointed at before. "The Futhark is the runic alphabet. Why do we call our alphabet the ABC?"

"Because it starts with A, B and C," I said.

"Exactly, and that's why the rune alphabet is called the Futhark. It starts with F, U, and so on. I would love to tell you that there's only one alphabet you need to learn, but sadly, there's the Elder, the Younger and a couple of other Futharks."

Kaycee sighed. "I wish I were in the standard class," she whispered. "I'd be happy to travel to the 1920s where everyone speaks English."

Maryam snickered and rolled her eyes. "Only if you're sent to an English-speaking country."

Hjalmar walked over and towered over Kaycee, staring her down. "Nothing is forcing you to be at the Academy," he said coldly. "You're free to leave if you're not interested."

A blush spread on her freckle-covered cheeks and she bowed her head and began to copy the Futhark alphabet into her notebook. I suppressed a grin, but couldn't help but smile when Hjalmar winked at me.

For the rest of the lesson, we learned about the runes that made up the Elder Futhark. Some of them were surprisingly similar to our own alphabet, others were deceiving and looked like one letter but meant another. X was actually a G and M was E. This was going to take a while to learn without getting confused.

"You'll be pleased to know that the basic Old Norse vocabulary isn't actually all that large. If you know the two-hundred-forty-six most frequent words, you'll understand eighty per cent of the sagas. Which is why I want you to know these words by next week."

Kaycee sighed, but she stayed quiet this time. She wasn't the only one depressed by this amount of homework. We'd only had one lesson so far and already, I was dreading my evening study periods. One week meant I had to learn thirty-five words a day, plus keep working on my rune writing. Why did I decide to go back to school?

Ah, yes. Time travel. I took the list of words Hjalmar handed me and looked at it with newfound enthusiasm. This wasn't just boring homework. This was preparation to travel into the past.

THE NEXT LESSON was in the big lecture theatre that I'd seen on the map. Once again, we were joined by the standard class of Hummingbirds, who Kaycee referred to as the 'pukers'. While we were waiting for a teacher to show up, I took out the map again. It was bugging me that I still hadn't figured out its strangeness. The lecture theatre was on the right side of the second floor, surrounded by classrooms on three sides. The wall to my right had to be an exterior one, but there were no windows to verify that. Now that I came to think of it, I hadn't seen a single window so far. Until now, I'd assumed that was because it was such a large building and most of the rooms I'd been in were closed in by other rooms, but that wasn't the case with the lecture theatre.

"Do you think we're underground?" I whispered to Maryam. "There are no windows."

Her eyes widened. "I hadn't realised."

"Neither had I. But look at the map, we're at the very edge of the building. And…"

The scales fell from my eyes. It had been staring right at my face. "There's no door," I muttered, staring at the map. "We arrived by porting, so we didn't need one. There wasn't a door leading outside from the entrance hall. There are none on the map. We can't leave this place."

It felt like a bucket of icy water had just been thrown at me.

"We're trapped," Maryam whispered, realising what I had just understood myself. "We can't port without cyber bracelets, so there's no way we could leave on our own."

"This is a prison." Kaycee was leaning over, having overheard our conversation. "That's crazy. They can't do that to us. We're here voluntarily."

"Hey girls!" Sue's cheery voice made us all jump. Our mentor slid into a seat next to Kaycee and grinned at us. "What's up?"

I wordlessly pointed at the map in front of me,

watching her closely. Sue's smile wavered a tiny bit, then she laughed.

"Figured it out, have you?"

"Is it true?" Kaycee asked, her voice shrill and verging on hysterical. "Are we prisoners? Are we trapped in here until you let us go?"

Sue almost choked on her laughter. "Prisoners? Why would you think that? If you want to leave, someone will port you to wherever you want to go. After a memory wipe, obviously."

"But what if I want to go for a walk?" I asked, claustrophobia settling into my mind. "What if I need some fresh air?"

"Honey, we're not keeping you here. But you can't go outside, nobody can. I couldn't port outside either, because there is no outside."

"No outside?" I asked. "Are we in space?"

She chuckled. "Might as well be. We're underground, far beneath the Earth's surface. It's the only way to keep our instruments shielded from all the waves and signals up there. There is nothing but earth and stone outside these walls. Definitely no way to go for a stroll."

Underground. Deep, deep underground. I suddenly felt pressure all around me, the earth trying to reclaim the part that had been ripped from her. Millions of tons of rock were waiting to crash down on us. No roof could sustain that pressure for long, right? We'd be crushed into dust.

"Hey, don't panic," she said and reached over to grab my hand. "We're safe here. Safest place on Earth, actually. If anything happens, we can port to wherever it's safer. Don't worry. The building won't collapse, no matter how afraid you are."

I looked at her, unable to keep the doubt from my expression. I'd never liked enclosed spaces and had been grateful that the bedroom I shared with Kaycee was large and spacious. Now, however, after realising that there was no air outside... I was having trouble breathing.

I gulped for air, clutching my throat.

"Oh my, are you having a panic attack?" Sue asked, suddenly not as cheery as she had before. "Ehm, let me get someone."

I squeezed my eyes shut, but that only made those old memories resurface, the ones I'd buried so deep that I barely remembered what had happened. The reason why I was claustrophobic. Why being in a building without a single window was a bad idea.

I tried to breathe, tried to count my breaths like my mother had taught me, but it wouldn't work. All I could think about was the lack of space, the threatening stone all around me. No air.

"Get her out of here."

I was pulled from my chair, but I was too busy trying not to scream. I was shaking all over. Even though I had my eyes closed, I could see stars exploding in the distance, bright lights that made me feel even more scared.

Someone had their arms around me, was leading me away, somehow making me walk even though I didn't know what I was doing. When a door fell shut behind us, the noise of the lecture theatre disappeared. I hadn't realised how much that noise had bothered me. Now that it was gone, my breathing became a little easier, but I was still having trouble not to scream and curl up into a ball.

But with the silence came the memories. *Locked away.*

Nobody there. All alone. No one can hear me. Nobody will come for me. I'll die here. Alone. In the dark.

I bent over, my stomach lurching, but I just about managed not to throw up. Acid filled my throat and I swallowed it, grateful for the pain that guided me back to reality.

"What's going on?" he asked. Hjalmar. It was him who'd brought me out of there. He still had an arm around my waist, supporting me. I wanted to step away, make it clear that I didn't need and want his help, but instead I soaked up his warmth, letting him ground me. He was real. He was here with me, underground. I wasn't alone this time.

"No doors," I managed to whisper, my voice hoarse and unsteady.

"Breathe," he reminded me. "Slow, deep breaths. Breathe with me. In..."

He put a hand on my chest and gently pushed.

"...out."

He pulled the hand away, leaving me with the sensation of a warm handprint on my skin.

"In... and out."

We stood like that forever. He never left, never stopped breathing with me. His hand became a fixture on my chest, reminding me of my task. Breathe. Calm down. Stay in the present.

"Open your eyes," he said softly.

I did, surprised at how easy it felt. He was looking down at me with concern, but there was warmth in his blue eyes too. He could have walked away, could have left me to deal with my demons all by myself. Instead, he stayed and helped me get through it.

This wasn't how a murderer behaved.

Turned out my Viking teacher had an actual office. Somehow, I hadn't put him down as the office type. Even having him teach felt strange. Like he was made to be running around outside, not bound by rules and social etiquette. Definitely not part of an Academy that was full of regulations and guidelines on how we were supposed to behave.

"Sit down," he said and pointed at a chair behind his desk. I did as he asked while he rummaged in a beautifully carved cabinet. A row of runes decorated the very top, but even if my Futhark knowledge had been better, I likely still wouldn't have been able to read it. I somehow doubted the runes were forming English words.

Hjalmar pulled out a bottle wrapped in paper and put it on the desk. It had been previously opened, there were stains on the paper, and there was no label to indicate what was inside. Even though I'd only known Hjalmar for less than a day, I didn't think it was going to be orange juice.

He pulled out two small glasses and handed me one.

My hand was still shaking, and I quickly sat the glass on the table before stuffing my hands in my pockets. Hjalmar followed my movement with his sharp gaze. I felt exposed under those watchful eyes of his, but in a good way. Like he was making sure I was okay. People didn't usually look at me this way. They just assumed that I had a handle on everything. Caring for my mother had given me a rough exterior, something that made others leave and stop offering to help. Hjalmar looked through that mask and saw the Lainie inside, who, right now, was terrified.

Just because I was breathing normally again didn't mean that the fear had disappeared. It still felt like an elephant was crushing my chest. I still had shivers run down my spine. All I'd managed to do was regain control over my body. Mostly.

Hjalmar poured us a drink. The liquid was honey-brown and thick. It didn't look particularly appetising, but when he handed me my glass, I poured it down my throat without hesitation. It was sweet, strong alcohol that coated my tongue at the same time as it burned its way down into my stomach.

"Just the way my dad used to make it," Hjalmar said with a nod towards the bottle. "It took me years to perfect the recipe."

I stared at him. "You made this?"

"Aye, every single drop. Want another glass?"

I nodded and immediately sipped on my refill. This stuff was delicious. I could get used to this.

"They say alcohol doesn't help solve your problems, but I think it can help to talk about them," he said softly. I didn't meet his eyes, instead preferring to stare at my glass.

"Why did you become so scared?" he asked. He was so gentle in the way he talked to me. I'd not expected that from him, not at all. Gone was the snarky humour, the mocking smirks.

I shook my head. "It's nothing. I just didn't like the thought of being trapped underground."

"We're not trapped. It may feel this way because you don't have a way to port to the surface yourself, but once you progress in your studies, you'll be given your own bracelets to let you port. You won't be stuck here forever."

He didn't get it, and why should he? This wasn't just a case of claustrophobia that would pass with a hug and a few nice words. It was much deeper than that, but it didn't concern him nor anyone else. Some burdens aren't for sharing.

"When?" I asked to distract both him and me. "When will we get bracelets?"

"In your second year. They don't trust you with them before." He chuckled. "As if you students become any more trustworthy over the course of a year. Accidents happen at least once a month. There's always someone who's overconfident or plain stupid."

An entire year until I would see the sky again. Until I could walk in fresh air. The pressure around my chest tightened.

"I can't do it," I whispered. "I need to leave."

"Look at me," he ordered. The gentle authority in his voice made me look up and meet his eyes. "You've been given an incredible chance here. You're one in a thousand who got the opportunity to study time travel, who'll be able to explore ancient cultures and walk with our ances-tors. Don't throw that away."

I shook my head. "You don't understand..."

"Then make me understand," he interrupted me, suddenly sounding a lot harsher. "Tell me. If it's a good enough reason, I'll take you home myself."

I sighed. "And if it's not?"

"Then you stay here, as my student. You're talented. I saw how quickly you understood the runes. Runology isn't just about learning how to draw the staves and put one rune after the other like letters. It's an art, a strange urge to arrange the runes to make beautiful words. Runes can be poetry, and I think you understand that already."

He downed his drink in one go and poured himself another. "I lost a talented student once. I'm not going to see that happen again."

I felt my heartbeat quicken. Was he referring to what the others had talked about? The student he took back into the past and murdered there? A slight doubt was nagging me again. Was it wise to be here with my teacher, drinking goodness what? It seemed like a terrible idea.

"Tell me," he repeated.

I stubbornly shook my head and looked back down at my empty glass. He hadn't offered to refill it. In a moment of pure dare, I took the bottle and set it to my lips, drinking greedily. It burned down my throat, making me cough, but I didn't stop. Only when I needed to breathe did I take a pause, which Hjalmar exploited to take the bottle from me.

"That was unwise," he said quietly. "You took some of what's precious to me."

I looked up at him in surprise. I hadn't intended it like that at all. It had been a challenge, maybe, or just something to distract him with. Not theft.

"Now I'm going to have to take something of yours,"

he whispered, his voice growing cold. "An eye for an eye. What's the price of a nostalgic moment?" He got up and walked towards the door. "A memory, I think." And he locked the door.

Panic flashed through me and I was up on my feet in an instant, trembling and swaying. I gripped the edge of the table, unwilling to sit back down even though everything was spinning.

"You're not going to leave this room until you've told me," he said, walking towards me until he was so close our bodies almost touched. He was towering over me, his body so much broader than mine. "Now sit down before you fall over."

His eyes were fire and ice, his expression full of threats and promises. I blinked up at him, trying to make sense of this strange man.

"Are you a Viking?" I blurted, the question forming on my lips before my mind could follow.

"I am," he replied with a shrug. "I thought you'd figured that out by now."

"Wanted to make sure," I mumbled, my tongue feeling heavy all of a sudden. "How... when..."

I let myself drop onto the chair, unable to formulate the question while fighting to stay upright.

Hjalmar chuckled. "Yes, I'm a Viking. Yes, I'm from the past. No, I'm not going to tell you why I'm here now and what led me to leave my home. And yes, this door stays locked until you face your fear."

Suddenly, the room seemed to grow dark. The walls moved, coming closer, ever closer, moving in rhythm with my heartbeat. I sucked in a breath, blinking several times, trying to make sense of what was happening.

"Tell me," he said for the third time. He was standing

behind me, I could feel his closeness even though he wasn't touching me.

I shook my head. "I've talked about it before. It doesn't make it better. It just makes it worse."

My words were slightly slurred, but I didn't care. I just wanted him to unlock the door so that the walls would stop moving and I could escape this place.

"Then you've been talking to the wrong people," he whispered, his mouth close to my right ear. "Tell me and I promise you will feel better."

Deep inside me, the memories were fighting against their chains. They saw the opportunity to rise to the surface, to torment me with all their might, and they weren't going to back down. I clenched my fists until my fingernails buried deep into my palms.

One of the memories, the strongest, burst free and shot up like a rocket, exploding in my mind, turning the present into the past.

"I was trapped," I say, my voice coming from far away. *Tell it like it happened to someone else,* I hear the therapist say in my mind. *Turn it into a story.*

"She was trapped," I start again. "Locked in a box. She was being punished. She couldn't remember what for. Her mother had told on her. Maybe her crime had been weeks ago. She didn't know. He didn't care about how long ago it was. He punished her anyway. He always did that when he came home."

In the distance, I feel Hjalmar take my hand, but I don't want to get distracted. I can only tell this story once.

"He locked her into the box for days. Like a coffin. She was hungry and thirsty. She needed to pee. She was scared of the dark and that's why he did it. It was so dark in that box. Dark and hot and stuffy. There was no space to sit up, so she had to lie the entire time, her legs bent. Her back started hurting because the wood was so hard. When she got out, she couldn't walk. She was dirty all over. She smelled and her mother called her names because she was so smelly. After she washed, she had to clean the box, for the next time."

"How often did they do that to her?" His voice was calm and flowed into the story. It was easy to answer.

"Whenever he came home. Every few weeks. He didn't like seeing her. She had to stay out of his way when he let her out."

"And when did it end?"

"When she started school. A child drew a picture of a cat in a box and she started crying. A teacher managed to find out what was happening. She was taken away and given to a nice woman who became her new mother. She never had to go into a box again, but she always stayed scared of small spaces."

"And now a teacher made you tell the story once again," Hjalmar said softly. I opened my eyes, not even sure when I'd closed them. He was kneeling on the floor, his hands gripping mine. I looked down at my lap, then back at him. I think he was waiting for me to push him away, to pull back my hands, but I didn't move. I met his eyes, surprised at the darkness swirling in his. A storm was brewing over the azure seas, a storm that I had conjured.

He gently rubbed his thumbs along my palms, easing the tension that had built there. I opened my hands, sore from having my fingernails pressing against my flesh.

"I'm going to prove to you that not every room

without a window is a prison," he whispered. "And I'm going to show you my home."

"Home? Don't you live here?"

He smirked. "My other home. I'm going to give you a taste of time travel, if you promise not to tell."

I grinned at him. I was good at keeping secrets. Except from him, apparently. The Viking who was quickly charming his way under my skin. Question was, would he turn away once he saw what was hiding inside of me? He'd only met one of my demons so far. There were many others waiting for him.

Only time would tell.

y runes were getting less shaky by the day. I was beginning to understand what Hjalmar had said about their own intrinsic magic. Deciphering a runestone filled me not only with a sense of achievement, but also with a strange feeling of connection, as if someone was speaking to me through those runes from the past. Even if it was just a gravestone that Hjalmar gave us a picture of, it felt strangely uplifting every time I managed to solve it.

I was nowhere near understanding all of the Old Norse texts he expected us to read though. While he was clearly a perfect man for the job, being a Viking and all, his teaching methods were lacking a little. He expected too much, too fast. For him, his subject was the most important of all, and he didn't care that we had a lot of other things to study at the same time. Knowing the two hundred and forty-six Old Norse words by the end of the first week made it easier to get a gist of what the texts were saying, but without knowing any of the grammar, it was hard to understand the details.

I'd certainly underestimated how hard this would be. And that was just the subject. Trying not to react to Hjalmar's smirks, mocking grins and amused glances was impossible. There was something between us, but I wasn't sure I wanted to explore it. He was my teacher, even though he rarely behaved like one.

We'd not spent any time alone since my panic attack last week. And yes, it was me avoiding him, not the other way round. As much as I had cherished his closeness, the way he'd touched my hands, the words he'd spoken to calm me, we had crossed a line that day. I'd given up far more of my secrets than I had ever wanted to share. Knowing that he *knew*... it made it hard to focus.

It took me two days to realise that I was ashamed. As much as it had helped to talk to him, it had also broken down barriers that should never have been touched.

I slid out of bed as quietly as possible. I was covered in sweat from the nightmare I'd had. The same one I'd had ever since I'd opened myself to Hjalmar.

I slipped out of the room and walked towards the bathrooms. There were no clocks anywhere nearby, but my inner sense of time told me that it was still a few hours until the morning bell would ring. I was going to be tired all day. I sighed. I needed to get a grip on those nightmares. Yesterday, I'd woken up Kaycee with my screaming. Luckily, she hadn't commented on it the next morning.

The bathroom was split into a row of shower cabins on the left and sinks on the right. I took some towels from a shelf at the entrance and headed to the shower at the very back of the room. I snickered. Even though I'd only been at TTA for a week, I'd already established a shower routine. Us humans really were creatures of habit.

I relaxed under the stream of hot water. The shower was powerful enough to knead the tense muscles of my shoulders and back. It washed away the nightmare, making it dissolve into a distant memory with every minute that I spent under the shower. Since I was alone, there was no rush to make way for others, so I only switched off the water when my skin turned red and wrinkly.

The towels here were always a little too rough, but the scratch of it helped push away the last of my tiredness. I was ready to start the day – except that I was probably the only person awake in the whole Academy. Breakfast wouldn't be served for some time yet. One thing I hated about this place. There was nowhere to get snacks, nowhere to make myself a cup of tea when I felt like it. In that way, it was like a prison, no matter how much Hjalmar tried to persuade me that it wasn't. Teachers had their own apartments at the top of the building, and I bet they could simply port to a shop and get however much chocolate as they wanted. I craved sugar. The food here was good, but it was restricted to three meals a day. I was used to snacking in between, and in the evening, and whenever I felt like it. This was a detox that I really didn't appreciate.

Food. Maybe I'd find something down in the kitchens. Maybe they weren't locked like I imagined. I smiled to myself and decided to turn explorer. Mission chocolate was about to begin.

I SHOULD HAVE KNOWN that both the kitchen and the dining hall were locked. So was the room I'd seen labelled as 'storage' on the map. Damn. So much for treating myself. The last few mornings when I'd woken up from nightmares, I'd used the time to study and revise. Time was precious at TTA, and yes, I got the irony of that sentence. Already, I wished I could travel back in time for a few hours so that I could use double the amount of study time. I'd never been an overachiever, never done more than was required to pass my courses, but here, that had changed. I *wanted* this. In high school, I'd never really had an aim, a purpose. Here, I knew exactly what I was studying for.

Vikings. I was going to meet Vikings. Real, fricking Vikings in the past. That was worth studying for.

It was strange walking through the Academy at night. My footsteps echoed in the stone corridors. Once again, I wondered how they'd built this place. We were deep underground, yet the architecture reminded me of a medieval castle. Take the massive marble columns in the entrance hall. Had someone ported the entire building underground? It seemed impossible but who knew what was possible with the TTA's technology. They still hadn't shown us the time travel equipment we'd be using, but I imagined it all to be very complex and complicated. Hopefully, we were going to find out soon. If Hjalmar was really going to take me into the past, I'd see how it all worked.

Now that food was out of the question, I had to find something else to occupy my time with. A strange tension was running through my body. I needed something to do. Something that wasn't studying. We'd been told we'd get physical training at some point, to help us defend ourselves, but so far, all the training we'd done had been for our brains.

Maybe I was tense because I hadn't been able to move much the past week. Back home, I usually went for a run every couple of days, mostly to get out of the house, but my muscles had got used to the regular exercise. Here, I was turning into a couch potato, minus the couch. I hated the plastic chairs in the common room. They weren't just uncomfortable, they also destroyed the atmosphere the beautiful stone walls created.

Since I was alone, I randomly started jogging down the corridor. I didn't have any trainers, but the shoes we'd been provided with were comfortable enough for running. The hallway I was running through formed a large square, encircling the large ground floor rooms. Because the building was so large, I got to run in a straight line for several minutes before having to turn.

I let my mind drift, enjoying the silence surrounding me. Silence had become precious. The Academy was always buzzing with students and staff, and with us not being allowed in our bedrooms until night time, there was nowhere to escape to. This was bliss. I decided I was going for a run every morning from now on.

Suddenly, someone was in front of me and we crashed to the floor, me mostly on top of him.

"Where the fuck did you come from?" he shouted as I tried to scramble away. He was a head taller than me with short black hair, eyes the colour of ash and a thin nose that reminded me of a hawk's beak. He wasn't pretty in the usual sense, but attractive in a strange, exotic way.

"I could ask you the same thing," I snapped back, looking around to figure out how he had suddenly appeared out of nowhere. There were no doors on this stretch of corridor, only stone walls with occasional portraits and tapestries. The light was too dim to see much detail, but I would have definitely noticed a door.

"Why are you up?" he asked in annoyance. "Everyone's supposed to be asleep."

"I'm awake, that's not a crime, is it?!" That man was riling me up for some reason. He'd disturbed my silence, my moment of peace, and now he was going to feel my wrath. Overdramatic? Hell yes. I was tired.

"It's not a crime, but why are you sneaking around here? You should be upstairs in your room."

I put my hands on my hips and glared at him. "Nobody has told me about a curfew. I have every right to be here. How about you just go about your business and leave me alone?"

"What do you know about my business?" he growled.

I looked at him in confusion. "Nothing. Should I? You've not exactly introduced yourself."

His eyes wandered over my uniform, focusing on my collar. I didn't have any coloured stitching there, making it obvious that I was a Hummingbird. With each year spent at TTA, you got one colour added to your collar. Then, after graduating, your rank was shown by how many silver earrings you had. Nobody had told us exactly what those were for yet, but I figured they were some kind of time travel technology, not just jewellery.

"You're new," he said, pointing out the obvious. "That's why you don't know who I am."

"So who are you?" I asked, beginning to think that I was missing something. If he assumed I'd know him, he had to be important, right? A teacher, maybe?

"I'm the Archivist," he said with a sigh. His anger was quickly flowing away, although his frown was still a little hostile. "I run the Academy's archive of historical artefacts. One of the most important jobs in this place. If people want to travel in time, they have to come to me." He shrugged. "I guess that's why I'm not used to anyone not knowing who I am."

"An archive? There's none on the map."

He chuckled. "Then you've not been given the right map. It's in the basement, taking up the entire floor. I think there's a tour scheduled for Hummingbirds in the next couple of weeks."

Excitement filled me. An entire level that I'd not known about? That meant there may be even more places to explore. Who was to say that there were only five floors? There could be many more, secret, ready for me to discover. Suddenly, I was feeling like an explorer, not one travelling through time, but one who was exploring the present.

"Can I see it?" I blurted. "The archive?"

His frown deepened. "You should be in bed. I'm busy."

I'd not really expected him to say yes, but at least I now knew that this archive existed. Maybe I could sneak down - if I found stairs leading to a basement. I'd not seen any so far, and they definitely weren't on the map.

He turned away, ending our conversation.

"Wait, what's your name?" I called out while he was already walking down the corridor.

"I told you, I'm the Archivist," he shouted back, his voice echoing through the stone hallway.

"That's not a name," I muttered to myself, but he'd already disappeared around a corner. I could still smell his scent. I hadn't realised how strong his cologne was while he was standing in front of me, but now that he was gone, I breathed it in.

Snap out of it, Lainie. What do you even see in that grumpy man? It's not like he was nice to you.

I rubbed the back of my neck. The tension I'd almost got rid of with my run was returning. I could continue running, but exhaustion was slowly taking over. I needed to build up my stamina again. It was as if a week of doing no exercise at all had ruined my fitness. Maybe I could ask at the student support office if I could have some train-ers. They'd already provided me with some additional notebooks.

I sighed and turned back, ready to head to my room again to collect my textbooks. Maybe I should have stayed there to do some homework after all. I still had to do an essay on the history of time travel. It was ironic that they made us study the history of it, but didn't actually tell us how it was done nowadays. Hopefully, we'd be taught that soon. I was impatient to learn all about it, especially after Hjalmar had talked about taking me to visit some Vikings. That would be crazy amazing. Which is why I didn't hold out hope. I didn't want to be disappointed. It was possible that he'd only mentioned it to get me out of my panic attack.

"I've changed my mind."

I swirled around, watching as the Archivist was hurrying back towards me.

"You can come along. I need help with something. Take it as your punishment for being out here at night."

"Punishment?" I protested. "I don't deserve any punishment. It's not a crime to be here. There's no rule for being out of bed, I've told you that before. I've read the rules many times."

He waved his hand dismissively. "Doesn't matter. I

need another pair of hands and you're here now. You're awake. That's what counts. Now come along, hurry."

He led me back to where I'd first stumbled upon him and stopped in front of a blank stretch of wall. The only thing that distinguished it from the rest of the corridor was that there were no paintings or tapestries. It was just... wall.

"Are you a ghost?" I asked jokingly. "You know, who can walk through walls?"

He only raised an eyebrow but didn't crack a smile. "You believe in ghosts?"

"No, but... never mind."

He pressed one of the large stone slabs that made up the wall and suddenly, not only this brick, but also several others bent backwards like a door. A secret passage? I should have known. This building hid many secrets.

So that's where he'd come from earlier. No wonder I'd run into him.

"Quickly, follow me and close the door behind you."

He disappeared into the narrow passage and after a moment's hesitation, I hurried after him, dutifully shutting the heavy stone door. It was almost as thick as the walls and I needed to push my entire body weight against it for it to move.

The corridor was dimly lit by a flimsy light bulb dangling from the ceiling. It highlighted a string of cobwebs lining the corners. Lovely.

I had to run to catch up with the Archivist, who was hurrying away with large steps. He was much taller than me and I had trouble keeping up.

I almost stumbled when the corridor turned into a steep set of stairs, leading down into the basement. I wondered why this wasn't on the map we'd been given. If we were going to be shown the archive soon anyway, why hide it?

I was glad when we finally entered a bright room looking like a big office. Far too big for the solitary desk in the centre of it. The walls were lined with bookshelves, hiding any trace of the stone walls. A door on the other side of the room was made from sturdy metal, looking like it was meant to either keep something in or out.

"Sit," the Archivist commanded and pointed at the chair in front of the desk. He himself sat on the only other chair and started rummaging around the papers on the table. There was no computer, just old-fashioned files and folders. For an academy dealing with the advanced technologies of time travel, this looked positively archaic.

"Something has gone missing from the archive," he said without looking up. "I didn't think I could trust anyone with helping me find it, but with everyone a suspect, you're ideal. You didn't even know this place existed, unless you're an excellent liar, which I doubt. Your face is an open book."

I glared at him. I prided myself at keeping my thoughts and feelings hidden from the world. Being called an open book was an insult that I took personal.

"What's gone missing?" I asked instead of heatedly disputing his accusation. It took a lot of effort. I was still tired and my self-control was at an all-time low.

"A ring. Tenth century, likely from Sweden. It's got some rather unique cut marks that may be faded runes."

"Viking?"

He nodded. "The archive is sorted by both historic and geographic origin. The Viking section isn't very popular since few people get to travel that far back, so I know exactly who's borrowed what. The ring hasn't officially been checked out, but it's disappeared. Someone took it without permission."

"Are there no security measures?" I asked.

The Archivist sighed in exasperation. "Of course they are. They somehow circumvented the detectors at the entrance. Only a few teachers and agents would have known how to do that, but none of them has a reason. Nothing prevents them from simply filling out a form to borrow Viking artefacts. Unless they've gone rogue."

I stared at him. "Why would they do that?"

"I don't know," he snapped, probably angry at having to admit that. "Nothing like this has ever happened before. Students regularly try to smuggle artefacts out of the archive, but the sensors help stop them before they get a chance to leave. Besides, I have an eye for spotting people who're up to no good. It's a complete mystery how this happened. But I need it back. The archive needs to be complete. We have a reputation to uphold. The archive has never been broken into before and if that becomes known, trouble will follow."

I nodded. "I get that, but what can I do to help? I've never even been in the archive. I don't know how things work."

"Don't they teach you anything nowadays?" He scoffed. "Come with me, I'll show you."

I hid a smile. I was going to see the archive after all.

The archive was big. Massive. Supersize. It filled the entire floor of the building, with shelves and racks as far as the eye could see. There had to be hundreds of shelves spread across the room in neat rows, disappearing into the darkness at the other end of the hall. The ceilings were low compared to the ones on the upper floors, but still higher than they'd been in our flat back home.

"Follow me, quickly," the Archivist said, once again hurrying away. Was he always in such a rush? I didn't think a few minutes more would make a difference in finding the ring.

I sighed and hastened to catch up with him.

"This corridor passes the archive in chronological order," he explained. "Here we have the most recent past, while the artefacts at the very end are all the way from the Neolithic period. Not that many people can travel there. A handful at most, everyone else would die trying to attempt a jump that far."

I swallowed hard. I hadn't realised it was that difficult to time travel into the past.

"Each row is then sorted by location. To the very left is Europe, then North and South America, and to the right are Australia, Africa and Asia. You'll see that while we have thousands of artefacts for the recent past, they will get more sparse the further we walk away from the entrance. Not all items from the past are suitable for time travel. They have to have a meaning, an emotional connection to its former owners. Jewellery and personal belongings work best, especially because they're small and easily carried during porting."

"How do you know if an item had an emotional connection?" I asked. "I mean, a ring we find now could have just been made by a blacksmith and not been used yet."

He nodded. "Good question. That's where I come in. I don't just look after our artefacts. I grade them, sort them, make sure they're suitable for time travel."

"How?"

"That's not for you to know," he replied with slight hostility. "Just trust me that all items in this collection are safe to use to travel in time."

"And we can just come and request one? Like a library?"

He chuckled. "Not if you mean 'we' to include you. No Hummingbirds are allowed to port, and Nightingales can only do it under supervision. You'll have to pass your Seagull tests before you can use the archive, and even then you'll have to submit to my opinion of you."

"Submit?" I muttered before I could stop myself. I didn't add how arrogant that sounded to me. How domi-nant. This guy was filled with self-importance. No wonder he worked alone down here.

"This is my archive. I make the decisions here." His tone was defensive, as if he'd had this conversation many times before. He pointed at the row we were passing. "This is the early nineteenth century. Not many people will travel much further than that."

"I'm in the fast track class," I blurted.

He stopped and looked at me curiously. "I didn't know we had one this year. How many of you are there?"

"Three."

"What do they teach you? What time period?"

My eyes widened slightly. Was it a coincidence? "Vikings. We're studying Vikings."

From his expression, I gathered that he didn't believe it to be a coincidence either.

"Every fast track class is assigned a different period," he said quietly. "That way, we can train experts in whatever area we're currently not having enough agents. Last year, it was medieval Europe, the year before the American Wars of Independence. For you to be assigned Vikings... that's further back than what's usually taught at Academy level. Anything earlier than the thirteenth century is normally studied after graduating from TTA. This is highly unusual."

I shrugged. "Maybe they've changed the curriculum?"

"They must have, but why? Vikings are interesting, but they're not important to any of the current Academy research. I've not heard of any new Time Agency missions that concern Norse culture either." He sighed. "More questions yet again. I shall have to make some enquiries. But here we are. The Viking section."

He turned left along a row of high shelves packed with metal boxes, probably to protect the artefacts. In some of the earlier rows, things had been in cardboard boxes and glass cabinets, but here everything looked much more secure. No wonder if what he'd said was true. Time travel to this period sounded dangerous. I was slowly realising how special that made our class. Just because we hadn't puked when we'd first ported. That seemed a strange criterion to go by. What if we simply had stronger stomachs? What if we were going to die on our first attempt to travel this far into the past?

"Why are none of the shelves labelled?" I asked as I hurried after him.

"To prevent people from taking things they shouldn't," he replied. "I know every single item in the archive. It's an extra layer of protection."

"But what if something was to happen to you?"

He turned around so suddenly that I bumped into him. He grabbed my arms and stared down at me. "Is that a threat?"

I looked at him in surprise. "No, just a question. If you're the only one who knows the archive, wouldn't that make it difficult if you fell ill or something?"

His grip softened a little, but he didn't let go of me. "I don't get ill," he said quietly. "It's one of the many perks of being the Archivist."

"Everyone gets ill."

He shook his head. "Not me. There are things you don't understand and I don't have the time to explain. Nor do I want to. You should be honoured that I've shown you the archive in the first place."

I bit back a heated reply that it had been him who'd asked for my help. He was a strange person, clearly anti-social and rude. Luckily, he finally stepped back, releasing his grip on my arms. We continued moving along the row of shelves.

"Why should I help you?" I asked defiantly. "I have homework and studying to do. What do I get out of it?"

He stared at me, his eyes filled with anger. "Seriously? Did you just ask if I'm going to pay you?"

"No, I didn't," I muttered, suddenly regretting my burst of overconfidence. "I just mean that I don't have much time. My schedule is packed and we only have Sundays off."

"What's more important, your studies or saving lives?"

I frowned at him. "How would finding a ring save lives?"

"If someone who's not trained uses that ring to time travel, they'll most likely die. Ergo, retrieving the ring will save the thief's life."

I found that a little far-fetched, but he was right in a way. Besides, it would be exciting, certainly more exciting than homework. But I was already struggling with keeping up with all my assignments, and this would only make it harder.

The Archivist sighed. "Tell you what, if you manage to help me find the thief, I'll help you with your homework. What you really need to graduate isn't what you find in books. It's first-hand experience. Learning by doing."

"You mean, I can learn to time travel with you?" I quickly closed my mouth when I realised I was openly gaping at him.

He chuckled. "No. That would be highly irregular, and besides, you need a lot more training before you can even learn to port from one place to another without even changing time zones. "What I can give you is the theoretical knowledge. The skill of how to choose the perfect artefact that's best suited to your intended journey. Most people have to figure that out by trial and error. I will be able to give you that information in exchange for your help."

I nodded. "Deal. How can I help?"

He stopped and turned to a shelf to our right. It was full of small metal boxes, many of them stacked into small towers. If he really knew every single artefact in this giant archive, this man had to have the brain of an elephant. I doubted I could even learn all the items in this row by heart, and those were just a tiny fraction of the complete collection. Crazy.

"This is where we store the Academy's Viking jewellery," he explained. "There's everything from necklaces to hairpins. The latter are particularly popular amongst female time agents, since they can be used both as a weapon, a lock pick and as jewellery."

My hair would never accept a hairpin. It was too thin, too slippery to even stay put in a rubber band.

He took a tiny box from the shelf and opened it. As expected, it was empty.

"That's where the ring was kept," he said, sadly eyeing the red velvet lining inside. "I discovered it was missing today, but it could have been stolen days ago. It was returned last week and I hadn't checked on it since then."

"What about fingerprints?" I suggested. "Are there cameras in here?"

He scoffed. "I already tried that. No fingerprints, they must have been wearing gloves. And we don't have cameras in the archive. This place is too important to have it on film."

I didn't quite get that argument, but I wasn't about to start arguing with him again. The way he looked at the empty box showed me that this was more to him than just a job. He took this theft personal.

"What now?" I asked. "How do I help?"

"Nobody knows that you're aware of the ring. Since you've not even been given a tour of the archive, the thief won't pay attention to you. If I went upstairs and started asking questions, the thief would know and make it even harder for me to find him."

"Or her," I interjected.

He sighed. "Or her. The ring was large though, so if the thief wants to wear it, they need to have large hands. It's more likely that it was a man. A woman may have chosen a smaller ring from our collection."

He closed the box and carefully put it back in its place.

"I need you to ask questions, make enquiries. Since you've been assigned Vikings, pretend it's for some research you're doing. As I said before, I doubt a student has stolen it, the ring would be of little use to them. It has to have been a teacher or a time agent. Or a student with a dangerous level of overconfidence."

I mulled this over in my head. "I can't just go to teachers and ask them whether they know of a specific ring," I said doubtfully. "Do you have a picture of it? So that if someone wears it, I can at least recognise it?"

The Archivist nodded. "Let's go back to my office. I'll show you the ring's file."

I followed him, now used to the speed in which he walked.

"Have you thought about scooters?" I asked when we were halfway through the large hall.

"Huh?"

"Scooters, or a segway, to make it faster to get to where you need to be. This room is so big."

He chuckled. "Nobody has ever complained about that before, but people rarely enter the archive themselves. Usually, they put in a request in advance and I get the artefact for them, and I enjoy walking through the archive."

He suddenly stopped and turned around. I barely managed not to bump into him.

"Can't you feel the call of history?" he asked, his eyes glowing with enthusiasm. "All the lives lived, the emotions felt while crafting these artefacts, the pull of wanting to explore the past?"

His passion was evident and I envied him for it. To me, this was a fascinating place, but I couldn't have been able to talk about feeling a pull or call without lying. Maybe that was because I hadn't travelled in time yet. It still felt like a dream to me, one that I was worried I might wake up from. Time travel wasn't something that ordinary people like me did. If I allowed myself to feel the same level of enthusiasm as the Archivist exhibited, then the pain of disappointment would be even greater.

His smile disappeared when I didn't answer immediately and he turned around with a sound of frustration.

"Of course you don't," he muttered and continued walking. Somehow, I regretted not telling him what he wanted to hear. It felt like I'd missed an opportunity to show him that I was worthy of his attention. But why did I even want that? Why did I want his praise? Why did I want to please him? I shoved away those thoughts. I was tired, that made me emotional and needy. This man was not someone I should get attached to. He was rude, demanding and, most importantly, not a fellow student. I already had questionable feelings about Hjalmar, that was bad enough.

Maybe I was getting my period. That would explain why I suddenly kept seeing hot men around me. Like the Archivist. Not that he was hot. Just different. Exotic. Exciting. Unusual.

I hastened my steps, trying to get rid of those thoughts. They were entirely inappropriate.

Just when we reached the metal door leading out of the archive, the morning bell rang. It sounded muted down here, nowhere near as shrill as it did in our bedrooms.

"I should go and get breakfast," I muttered when we entered his office.

He nodded, not meeting my gaze. Again, I had the distinct impression that I'd disappointed him.

"Let me show you the ring first," he said and took a tablet from a desk drawer. He switched it on using a fingerprint sensor, then turned slightly so that I couldn't see what he was doing.

It was almost reassuring that he did use some kind of technology. When I hadn't seen a computer earlier, I'd assumed that this archive was stuck in the past somehow. Having a record of the archive in electronic form made it a little easier to believe his claim that he knew every artefact in the collection.

"Here it is." He swiped his fingers over the screen and a hologram formed above it, showing a beautiful golden ring. It had heavy signs of use, with scratches all over, but what made me step closer were the marks carved on the inside and outside of the ring.

"What do they mean?" I asked, staring at them in wonder. They were tiny, delicate; I doubted anything bigger than a needle could have created them.

"Nobody knows," the Archivist replied. I felt his gaze

on me, but I didn't look up, keeping my eyes focused on the ring. "They look like runes, but they're nothing like the ones we know about. Maybe it was a secret language the creator or the owner of this ring used. Maybe it was just a strange way to decorate it. We don't know."

"Have you shown it to Hjalmar? He might know."

"Hjalmar?" he asked with a chuckle. "The Viking? Sounds like you haven't heard about his past yet, or you wouldn't talk about him in such a familiar way."

I met his eyes, staring at him defiantly. "I've heard the rumours, but I don't believe what they say. He's not a murderer."

The Archivist started laughing. "Oh dear, that he certainly is. He was known as the Red Sword in the old days. One of the finest warriors of his time. He killed for a living, so I'm pretty sure that makes him a murderer."

I glared at him, but there was truth to his argument. If Hjalmar really had been a warrior. He did have the physique for it, but maybe all Vikings had abs like his.

The bell rang for a second time.

"I have to go," I said quickly before he could tell me any more things about Hjalmar that I didn't want to hear. "I'll tell you if I find something."

"I'll be waiting," the Archivist said quietly, but loud enough for me to hear. There was a certain sadness to his words, as if he was used to waiting. To being alone down here in the archive.

Well, once I'd found the ring, he was going to help me with my studies. That might make him less lonely. I smiled at the thought, before remembering that he was a grumpy prick.

CHAPTER 8

I barely tasted breakfast, and my first lesson in Time Travel Law passed without me making a single note. To be honest, I wasn't really interested in this, especially after the teacher had actually said in last week's lesson that common sense and morals prevailed in most cases. But still... I had planned to be a good student to get the grades I needed. It was hopeless though. My head was full of the Archivist, his ashen eyes, the impossible mission he'd given me.

Instead of listening to my teacher drone on about medieval law and punishments – basically, whatever you did was punishable by death – I made a plan of how to solve the mystery of the stolen ring. My first task was going to be talking to Hjalmar. While I knew there were other Viking experts and teachers, he was the only one I'd had a proper conversation with.

I rubbed the palms of my hands with my thumbs, remembering his gentle touch. A blush heated my cheeks. I shouldn't savour this memory. It was wrong, so wrong. I should stay away from Hjalmar before this strange attraction got me in trouble – but that was impossible. He was my teacher, I was going to see him at least three times a week in lessons.

Maybe I should just go to him and ask him outright about the ring. I doubted he could have been the thief, and he might have some leads for me. He knew the other TTA Viking agents.

But did I really know him well enough to discard him as the thief? He had a clear distaste for rules, that much was clear after attending his lessons. He refused to stick to the curriculum, instead deciding to teach what he thought was most important to keep us alive during missions. I didn't have a problem with that in the slightest. Staying alive sounded like a good idea.

"Lainie, what do you think of the Iron Maiden as a punishment?"

Miss Long's voice almost made me jump.

"Ehm... terribly inhumane?" I stuttered, just about remembering the strange metal sarcophagus I'd seen in a museum, where poor buggers would be gruesomely stabbed to death.

"Since you're obviously too busy to listen to my lesson, I want you to write a two-thousand-word essay about how the Iron Maiden was a Victorian invention. By tomorrow."

I groaned internally. As if I didn't have enough to do already. It had only taken a week for me to get extra assignments. Damn it. I should never have agreed to help the Archivist. It wasn't going to be good for my studies.

Luckily, the bell rang before Miss Long could humiliate me any further. I fled the classroom, walking to Hjalmar's office as fast as I could. We had five-minute breaks in between lessons, so hopefully, he'd still be in his office. He was late for lessons quite frequently.

"Hjalmar!" I shouted when I saw him step out of his office. I ran to him, ignoring the curious stares both students and teachers gave me. One teacher next to Hjalmar cleared his throat and I quickly added a "Sir". The teacher nodded, satisfied, and walked away.

"I like it when you call me Sir," Hjalmar muttered under his breath. My cheeks flamed red hot. What was I getting myself into? I was playing with fire, no, with a blazing Viking axe that could sever all my hopes of ever becoming a time agent.

He stepped back into his office and I followed him, unwilling to meet his mocking gaze.

"What is it?" he asked, leaning against the edge of his desk. As always, his shirt was unbuttoned more than it was appropriate for a teacher. I could almost see his hard chest muscles underneath, with the way the fabric stretched. He needed to get larger shirts, the ones he wore were far too tight. Like he wanted to tease the entire female population of the Academy. Evil Viking.

"I need to talk to you," I spluttered, staring at the floor, away from his taunting chest and his mocking eyes. This man was going to be the death of me. And of my career, if I wasn't careful.

"Well, you're in my office, talk. Unless talking is code for something else." He chuckled and my cheeks grew even hotter.

"I was wondering, when you travel back to Viking times, do you need artefacts like other people?" I asked quickly, thinking on my feet.

He frowned at me. "That's what's so important? You could have asked that in class."

I shrugged. "Do you?"

"No, unless I want to travel to times before I was born, or to places I didn't visit. There's no reason for me to do that just now, so I don't think I've used an artefact in years. Why are you asking?"

Relief filled me. The thief couldn't be Hjalmar, which meant I was able to confide in him. That would make my mission a lot easier. Although I was beginning to wonder why the Archivist hadn't talked to Hjalmar himself. Surely he knew that my Viking hadn't borrowed an artefact from the archive in years?

Fuck. Did I just think 'my' Viking? I wanted to beat my head against the wall. This was getting ridiculous.

"This has to stay between us," I said and he nodded, pushing himself off the desk. He was close now, in my personal space. His breath tickled my skin, giving me all sorts of sensations that I was trying my hardest to ignore.

"I can keep a secret," he promised. His voice had changed, the mocking tone gone.

"I'm helping the Archivist with something," I began. "A Viking ring has gone missing and he's tasked me to find out who may have taken it. He thinks it was a teacher or time agent, not a student. And since you don't need artefacts to time travel... Can you help me?"

I looked up at him, meeting his eyes. His gaze was intense as always, his blue eyes boring into me, looking right into my soul. I didn't like what he might find there.

Suddenly, he began to laugh. He threw back his head in laughter, while I stared on, unsure of what was happening. A pang of disappointment tore into my heart. I'd thought he'd help me. That he cared enough to not see this as a joke.

"I'm glad that this is amusing you," I snapped after he

didn't stop laughing. "But if you don't want to help me, we better go to class."

He put a hand on my shoulder, stopping me.

"You want me to help you with finding that ring?" he asked, still chuckling.

I shook off his hand. "I did until you started making fun of me."

He roared in laughter. Fine. I was not going to let him do this to me. I turned and put a hand on the doorknob, when suddenly, a knife whizzed past me and embedded itself inches away from my hand.

"What the fuck?!"

I turned around, only to see him lazily playing with another knife, turning it in his hand in a dangerous way that made me wonder how he managed not to cut himself.

"Did you just threaten me?" I asked, lost for words. He'd thrown a knife at me!

Hjalmar shrugged. "That's how you interpret it. I see it as gently stopping you from leaving so that I can explain to you why I find it so amusing."

I glared at him. "Then explain."

He grinned devilishly. "I'm the thief."

"What?"

"Did the knife hit your ears? I took the ring. You're looking at the thief. Well done for solving this crime so quickly." He snickered and I was tempted to pull out the knife and throw it at him. If I'd known how to do that. We were going to have self-defence lessons soon, but I doubted they would involve learning how to throw a knife at a teacher.

"But why?" I asked, trying to hide my disappointment. And here I'd thought he was an almost decent human being. Not who everyone else took him for. "You said you didn't need artefacts to travel. Why would you take it?"

He winked at me, making me even more furious. Until he said, "For you. I promised you a trip to my home, didn't I?"

I gaped at him. "For me?"

"Even when travelling in groups, everyone needs an anchor to get them to the right destination. Since you're a Hummingbird, nobody would have given you a Viking item, least of all that stickler of an Archivist. Taking it seemed like a good idea at the time."

I leaned against the door, the fight knocked out of me. What the hell was I supposed to say to that? And what was I to do? I couldn't tell the Archivist that I'd been complicit in the theft, even though it had been unknowingly.

"You stole a ring for me," I stuttered.

Hjalmar laughed. "It's not like it's an engagement ring, so you can stop blushing."

I touched my cheeks. He was right, they were hot again. Or still. I seemed to do a lot of blushing in his presence.

"Since you now know my little surprise, how about we go on a trip to my home?"

"Now?"

"Anything stopping you? We'll be back in time for our lesson." He groaned. "Which I forgot to prepare."

Despite myself, I laughed. He really wasn't a natural teacher. He was passionate about his subject, obviously, but he wasn't very good at turning his knowledge into lessons.

"I've never done this before," I blurted, excitement

and apprehension mixing in my voice. "I don't know how to do it. What if I make a mistake?"

He smiled at me; a genuine, friendly smile. "That's what I'm here for. I've been time travelling for longer than you can imagine, so I know a thing or two about it. You'll be fine, don't worry."

"But I don't even know what kind of technology is used for travelling. Is it a machine? A portal? The same thing as porting? We've not been taught any of it yet."

I knew I was rambling, but excitement and worry got the better of me.

Hjalmar began to laugh again. "Don't worry, I won't let anything happen to you. I'll show you everything step by step. It's not as hard as everyone makes it sound. The main reason they don't let students time travel right away is that they want you to focus on your studies first. Have an incentive to do all your assignments."

"So it's not as hard as they say?"

He shook his head. "Granted, it requires focus and a certain measure of control, but with a bit of help, every idiot could do it. Of course, the Academy would never admit that. People would want access to the technology if they knew that four years of study isn't technically necessary to time travel." He chuckled. "They forget that it's not all about the actual travelling. There's a reason why you're studying languages, culture, laws, all that. The further back you go in history, the more likely you are to be mistaken for a witch or a deity. Trust me, neither of that ends well."

The bell rang, interrupting him. He looked at his watch with a sigh. "Maybe we should do the lesson first. As much as I want to show you my home, I need to hold this lesson. I've been told an inspector is going to pay me a surprise visit soon, so I better be at my best behaviour." He groaned. "I should never have agreed to his plan. It's put me in all sorts of trouble."

"His plan?" I asked in confusion.

"You'll see soon. Now let's go, we've got some more runes to look at."

ᚠᚾᛒᛁᛏᚢᚠᛚ 9

The lesson passed faster than ever before. No inspector came and with every minute that passed, Hjalmar became more relaxed. It was obvious that he was dreading the inspection. Was it routine or related to that murder rumour?

"As homework, I want each of you to interpret the runestone I'm about to show you. Here's a spoiler: it's a gravestone. But what's important isn't the name of the man buried there, but the circumstances. Who buried him? Who commissioned the stone? Why did he die where he died? You'll find some of the clues in the inscription, but others will require a bit more research."

Kaycee groaned loud enough for Hjalmar to shoot her an annoyed look.

"Kaycee, three thousand words for you. Maryam, two thousand for you. Lainie, you're going to help me with something instead; I'll count that as practical course-work. Although you're of course free to write a detailed essay about the stone as well, if you want to."

He winked at me at the same time as Maryam whispered, "Are you sure this is a good idea? I don't like the way he looks at you."

"It's fine," I muttered beneath my breath. "He's not the bad guy everyone thinks he is."

"That's not what I'm worried about," she whispered. "But if you end up sleeping with him, it might affect your studies, let alone your career. Is it worth that?"

"I'm not planning on sleeping with him," I protested a little too loudly.

"You're not?" Hjalmar asked from behind.

Ground, swallow me up whole! I'd not even realised that he'd left his seat behind the teacher's desk and moved around. Damn it. How could I ever look at him again? Without dying, I meant.

Kaycee snickered. "I'd do it," she whispered, clearly not caring in the slightest that Hjalmar might hear her. "He's hot."

"Four thousand words," Hjalmar said to Kaycee and she winced. "Now that the homework is sorted, Lainie, come with me. And no, there won't be any sleeping involved."

He left the room before any of us could say something. I was left with my two classmates staring at me with both confusion and pity.

"What is he up to?" Maryam asked.

"I don't know," I lied. I couldn't tell her that he was about to give me my first taste of time travel. It was against school rules and it was bad enough that I was even considering it.

"Well once you're done, you can help me with this essay," Kaycee grumbled. "Unless he's fucked your brains out."

I threw my pencil case at her, but she was too fast and

snatched it out of the air before it could hit her face. Maybe I should ask Hjalmar for some knife throwing lessons. But no. Even more extra-curricular contact with him was a bad idea.

I quickly packed up my things and hurried after Hjalmar, correctly predicting that he'd returned to his office. He was leaning against his desk once more, now wearing the cyber bracelets used for porting.

"Are they used for time travel too?" I asked before I could stop myself.

"Partly. We need them to port into the time stream, but from there, it's back to old school focus and determination. And the artefact, obviously."

"Obviously," I muttered, not entirely convinced that I was going to be able to pull this off. I had no idea what I was doing. Porting itself sounded like enough of a challenge, and what the heck was the time stream?

He put a hand on my arm and I looked up at him. "Don't worry. I'm going to be with you the whole time. It's not as difficult as everyone makes it sound. Although if you're scared, we don't have to do it." His eyes betrayed his words. He wanted this and he was going to be disappointed in me if I said no. Besides, who was I kidding? I wanted this too. My anxiety wasn't going to stop me.

"Let's do it," I said, straightening my back and squaring my shoulders. My mum always said that changing your body posture also helped change your mental attitude.

He took a pair of bracelets from the desk behind him.

"I've programmed them to sync with mine," he explained as he handed them to me. "They'll do exactly what mine do, so you won't have to do anything yourself to port." He cleared his throat. "You didn't puke, did you?"

I shook my head.

"Good. I don't fancy arriving in my home village covered in vomit. Now put them on so that they're tight on your skin. Tight enough to be almost painful."

The silver-coloured bracelets were about as wide as my palm and surprisingly heavy. They were big enough to easily slip over my hands, but as soon as they touched my wrists, they tightened. I barely managed to pull back my fingers. A sharp pain shot through my left wrist.

I gasped and Hjalmar chuckled. "I should have probably mentioned that. The bracelet takes a DNA sample when you first put it on."

I winced, wanting to rub the sore spot but unable to do so because the bracelet covered it. "Is that so it can put me back together after I've been splintered into a million atoms?" I asked drily.

"You've got a fascinating imagination, but no, it's just to make sure nobody else can use them until you voluntarily take them off. We wouldn't want someone in the past to use them to travel to the present. Oh, and they also track you, should you get lost. Not that's that a possibility. I'll be with you the whole time." He grinned at me, wiggling his eyebrows. "Even if you're not sleeping with me."

I groaned. "About that..."

"Here's the ring," he cut me off. "It's probably too large for you, so put it on your thumb. Once we're there, my brother can make it smaller for you. He's a smith."

"You've got a brother?"

"Aye, Asger. He's a year younger than me but he likes to pretend he's older. He's all settled down, you see? Got his own forge, a house, a share in a boat. The only thing that's missing is a wife." He chuckled. "He's driving our mother crazy. She keeps introducing him to eligible women, but he ignores them all. Says the right woman for him hasn't been born yet."

I took the golden ring and put it around my thumb as he'd suggested. It fit perfectly. The strange markings inside gave it a good grip.

"Do you know what the markings mean?" I asked, remembering how even the Archivist hadn't known.

"No, but I'm planning to ask my brother. I have a suspicion, which is why I chose this ring and not one of the smaller ones that would have fit you better. I'm sure my father would have known, but he now lies in Hel's embrace."

"I'm sorry," I said, glad he'd taught us about Hel in a previous lesson. Hel was the daughter of Loki, responsible for looking after those who'd died of old age or sickness. He'd mentioned that there were a lot of sexual connotations around death, like the newly deceased sleeping with Hel after having feasted at her table. He'd told us to look up funeral rituals that incorporated sex, but I'd not had the time yet. And I hadn't wanted to think of anything remotely sexual with him as my teacher.

Even though the word Hel sounded like hell, it wasn't a place of punishment. Still, most Vikings preferred to end up in Valhalla or with the goddess Freyja in Fólk-vangr, realms reserved for those who'd died in battle. Even though I'd only just scratched the surface of learning about Norse culture, it felt both alien and familiar at once.

"If you don't mind me asking," I said quietly, "do you

believe in all the Viking mythology? I mean, after living here, your beliefs may have changed?"

He stared at me, clearly taken aback. "No one's ever asked me that before," he said after a moment's hesitation. "I think they all assume that because I wear modern clothes and have almost lost my accent, I've left behind all of the culture I was born into. But yes, I still hold onto my beliefs. I hope that one day, I will end up in Helgafjell, the holy mountain where the wine never runs dry and the food never gets cold."

"Not Valhalla?" I interrupted and he shot me a grin.

"There are no women in Valhalla, only Valkyries. No, I don't want to be celibate for the entirety of my afterlife. Helgafjell is where the party's happening. And hopefully, I'll still be able to train there for the final battle."

"Ragnarök?"

He nodded. "The battle of Gods and men, when the world will fall only to be reborn again. But let's not waste time, we can talk about all this when we're home."

He handed me a silver earring. "That's the translator. Put it in and it'll stream the words straight into your mind. But remember what I said, the translations are very literal."

I put it in, glad I had holes in my ear lobes. I very rarely wore jewellery nowadays, but I had back when I was a teenager, trying to impress the boys. Not that it had worked.

He lifted his arm and a hologram appeared above his bracelet. He did a lot of complex finger motions, distorting a web of lines that apparently was some sort of data input. It would have been much easier to simply enter a destination, but I guessed simple wasn't in TTA's vocabulary.

"Hold your bracelet against mine," he ordered. When I did, the same hologram appeared on mine, followed by a gentle vibration. "They're synced now and set to take us into the time stream. From there, our artefacts take over."

"What's yours?" I asked.

He grinned and beat a fist against his chest. "My blood, my connection to my brother and mother. As long as they're alive, I don't need a physical artefact to guide me home. I do have one, just in case, but let's hope I will never have to use it. Thanks to being part of TTA, I'll be able to send a present-day doctor to my mother should she ever be in need of one. As much as she misses my father, I won't have her join him and Hel any time soon."

I wanted to ask more questions about how he'd be able to explain a modern doctor appearing in a village full of Vikings, but my bracelets began to vibrate harder until I had trouble keeping my wrists steady.

"This will work best if we touch," Hjalmar said with a smirk. "Do you want to face me or shall I hug you from behind?"

"Hug?"

He chuckled. "The more we touch, the better. Hugging is a great tool for time travel."

I looked at him doubtfully. Was he making this up in order for him to get close to me? Not that I minded... No, I did mind. I needed to stay away from him, and he from me.

"Don't we need to change clothes?" I asked to play for time. "Put on something more appropriate for the time period?"

"My brother has all that and we'll be able to borrow clothes for you from my mother. I don't have any female clothes here, unless you want me to steal some from the archive?" He snickered.

"How did you even do that?"

"Trade secrets. As a time agent, you automatically become a spy. Even though I now work as a teacher, I got the full training. Including how to infiltrate enemy buildings behind several layers of security." He shrugged, his expression full of mirth.

"I bet they didn't count the archive as an enemy building," I said, barely managing to hide a grin.

"A matter of interpretation. Now, how shall we touch?"

I sighed. "From behind."

I didn't want my mouth to be anywhere close to his. There was too much temptation in those curved lips, the beard surrounding them, the masculine scent I couldn't get out of my nose.

I turned, waiting for him to touch me. A shiver ran down my back when he gently stepped closer, his chest touching my back. I'd not been this close to a man in forever. Ever? I'd played around with boys back at school, but I'd never gone beyond snogging and a bit of curious fumbling. And once I'd left school, I'd cared for my mum day and night, leaving little time for a social life, let along dating. All the experience I had came from books, and I doubted that they were very realistic. Granted, I did have an actual Viking pressing his body against mine, which did sound like a scene from a book, but it wasn't in that way. Not romantic. Just practical. To jump in time.

He wrapped his arms around my waist and another shiver made my gooseflesh rise. My body was reacting to him in ways that I couldn't control.

"Ready?" he whispered into my ear, his breath hot on my neck.

I nodded. I didn't really feel ready, but I doubted I ever would.

"See you in the past," he muttered and before I could even take another breath, we were ripped into sunlight.

I was old and young and everything in between. I knew everything and nothing. My life ended before it began, only to begin again and again. Time was endless, existing between the lives it touched, hugging us like a mother her newborn.

Hjalmar was all around me. I sensed him, his past, his future. He shared with me memories that he himself no longer remembered, and I knew that he could see my past as well as I could see his. Our minds merged, separated, merged again. His touch became my touch, and through it, our bond increased.

We were one being split into two bodies.

It was painful to let go of time. Stepping from perpetual infinity into the confinements of a present - a new present - was like being ripped apart. Only his touch kept me sane.

We arrived curled around each other. For a moment, I wasn't sure where I ended and he began. I stayed in that position, unwilling to confront the fact that something had happened that I'd not expected. Hjalmar was no longer a stranger to me. It felt like I had always known him. Like I knew him better than I knew myself. I knew his favourite colour (the blue of the sea at midnight), his favourite food (bacon so crispy it was almost burned) and the way he liked to touch himself in the show-

"What was that?" I muttered, still not moving.

"I don't know."

Without opening my eyes, I knew exactly how he was curled around me. I knew that he was looking at the beauty spot on my chin, I knew that he was fighting the urge to press his lips against mine.

"Do it," I whispered before I could stop myself.

He didn't hesitate. He kissed me and I kissed him, somehow feeling both my own and his lips as if they were mine. It was confusing and yet oh so amazing. I'd never been kissed like that before. His beard chafed against my skin, but I loved the way it felt, how it made his lips feel soft and gentle compared to the harshness of the other sensation. He made me open my mouth with nothing more than a thought, and his tongue met mine, desperately trying to find each other. We were close, touching, kissing, yet not as close as we had been moments ago when we had been one and the same.

Our kiss turned wild, all gentleness gone. We devoured each other, a dance more battle than beauty. His taste was raw, filled with the iron of blood. One of us was bleeding, maybe both of us, but it just added to the frenzy that filled my mind. I needed more of him. All of him.

I fumbled with the zipper of my jumpsuit, so distracted by the kiss that it took me forever to open it. I slid out of the sleeves and pushed the suit down until my upper body was bare. Without stopping the kiss, Hjalmar reached around me and opened the clasp of my bra in one practised motion. His tongue swirled around my mouth one last time, then he left my lips, drawing his down my chin, my neck, until he started kissing the soft skin between my breasts. I moaned at the gentleness of his touch, the careful placement of the kiss right atop of my centre. My heart was beating fast, aching to jump out of my chest and into his.

That strange sense of being one and the same was still there, although it was fading quickly, far too quickly. It was still strong enough to feel his arousal though, and that turned me on even more. His cock pressed against my hip, but the desire in his mind was so much stronger. Enough to almost bring me over the edge before I'd even completely undressed. Before he'd touched me where I wanted him to touch me.

I was quivering beneath him as he placed kiss after kiss on the small space between my breasts. His beard tickled my skin, while his hands were moving down, grabbing the jumpsuit and pulling it down. One of his hands pushed between my legs, sliding underneath my panties. He wasn't going to wait, he was going to take me here and now, I could feel it in his thoughts. I was okay with that. More than okay. I craved him like the air that I now breathed in short, ragged breaths. I'd felt his mind merge with mine, now I wanted the same to happen to our bodies. Have him inside of me.

That thought alone made me squirm. His mouth was moving over to my right breast, his lips gently hugging my nipple. He began to suck just enough to stretch the skin but not enough for it to hurt. I wanted him to be less gentle, but I couldn't remember how to speak.

I moaned as he pushed a finger inside of me, giving me a taste of what I needed. His thumb stroked my clit in slow circles. I pushed up my hips to meet his touch. I wanted more. It wasn't enough.

He moved onto my other breast at the same time as a second finger joined the first. Already, I was close to being too full. I had no idea how his cock was going to fit into me if two large fingers already made me feel like this. Still, I wanted it. He could take my innocence, I gave it to him freely.

Suddenly, Hjalmar roared in pain. I opened my eyes and his fingers slid out of me, all pleasure gone immediately as fear gripped my heart. I felt my own wrists burn as he pressed his against his chest, agony marring his features. His bracelets were showing the same line hologram again as they had back at TTA. He wasn't doing anything to them, but the lines kept swirling, moving into a new pattern. My stomach lurched as I realised what was happening a second before it did.

Hjalmar was wrenched from my grip before either of us had the chance to say something.

Say goodbye.

I was holding nothing but thin air. The man in front of me had gone, disappeared into time.

I was alone, trapped in a Viking village, imprisoned in a past I'd never lived.

"Hjalmar," I whispered, shock slowly giving way to tears.

Without warning, my bracelet vibrated and fell off my wrists. I stared at the silver pieces of metal, wishing them all the harm in the world.

They weren't going to help me go back. I wasn't going to be able to travel back home.

No, the only thing I could do was wait.

Wait for Hjalmar to return. To bring me home. To make me his for real.

I stumbled out of the barn we had landed in. My white uniform was covered in straw, but even without the jumpsuit I would have stood out like a sore thumb. I was in a Viking village, in the past, without Hjalmar to guide me. What the fuck was I going to do now?

There was a house next to the barn, although hut would have been a more accurate description. Nothing big and fancy, just a purpose built dwelling. The walls were curved inwards, reminding me of a ship's bow riding through a sea of thatch. Hjalmar had mentioned a brother. Was this Asger's house? It would make sense that we'd landed in the barn next to his home, although I wasn't sure how accurate time travel was. Could you choose the exact location you landed? Or was it more of a game of luck?

I took a deep breath. I was stuck here for now, and hiding in the barn wouldn't do me any good. I had no idea when Hjalmar would return. Because he was going to come back. I refused to think of the alternative. But it could be days or weeks. I needed food and suitable clothes and shelter and...

I pushed all those thoughts from my mind and instead focused on my knowledge of Old Norse. And realised I had no idea how you even said 'hello'. Had that been part of the two hundred something words I'd learned? I didn't think so. Maybe they hadn't greeted each other a lot in the sagas. The vocabulary we'd been taught so far hadn't been chosen to prepare us for having small talk with Vikings. I guess we weren't supposed to even meet any of them until much further into our studies. I wasn't ready. I may have used my knowledge of runes if there'd been a sign in runic writing, but no such luck. It seemed Vikings didn't have house numbers or signs with their names on. It would have been too easy.

Alright. There was no way around it. I walked to the door and knocked. Was that even what you did here? Or should I have just walked in confidently? Somehow, I didn't imagine Vikings to be the knocking type, but maybe that was because the only Norseman I knew was Hjalmar, who didn't have any manners and was plain rude most of the time.

The door opened before I could think more about what to do, revealing a brute of a man. The sleeves of his simple linen shirt were rolled up, revealing massive arms, probably strong enough to squash my skull without much effort. He wasn't as tall as Hjalmar, but quite a bit broader. Soot stained his skin not just on his arms, but on his face too. His blond beard was full of ash as well. Bright blue eyes stared at me from beneath bushy eyebrows. Very familiar eyes. This had to be Asger.

His gaze wandered up and down my body, sending a shiver running down my back. He had the same intense stare as his brother. His eyes widened the longer he looked at me, as if he was surprised by something.

"Hjalmar?" he asked after a moment, his voice deep and rough. He pronounced the name in a strange way, making me realise that I must have pronounced it wrong the entire time. And my stupid Viking never corrected me once.

I shook my head, but didn't know what to say. "Eigi.... heðra..."

He started laughing loudly, throwing his head back in amusement. I sighed, hopelessness spreading in my chest. I'd tried to say 'not here', but it seemed I had failed. Miserably. If I couldn't even say something that simple, I had no hope of communicating with the people in this village. Would they see me as an enemy?

He winked at me, then turned and roared, "Lucas!"

That wasn't a Viking name, right?

Shuffled footsteps announced someone approaching moments before a young man appeared behind Asger. He stared at me with wide eyes.

"Future?" he asked in perfect English.

I nodded.

A grin spread across his face, and suddenly he launched at me, pulling me into his arms. Startled, I let him hug me, totally confused about what was happening. He squeezed me tight, holding onto me like a drowning man onto a log.

"I didn't think he'd make good on his word," he muttered. His breath was hot against the nape of my neck. I couldn't help but note his scent; earthy with hints of smoke. I'd never had a chance to look at him properly, but I bet his clothes were stained with soot just like

Asger's. Hjalmar had mentioned that his brother was a smith. Lucas, whoever he was, had to be helping him out.

When I felt he'd been hugging me for long enough, I gently pushed him away.

"Who are you?" I asked, not able to hide a smile. He spoke English! I could communicate with him!

He returned the smile, then wiped his eyes. Was he crying?

"Let's go inside and talk there," he said instead of an answer. He turned and walked away, leaving me with an amused looking Asger. The Viking pointed at the door and said something I didn't understand. I frowned, remembering that I should be able to know what he'd said. I touched my translator earring. Nothing happened. Maybe it was broken, just like the bracelet.

I followed Asger inside. My eyes started tearing up when smoke hit me. Was the forge inside? No, it was just a fire, but since there were no windows, the only way the smoke could escape was through a hole in the roof. Benches circled the fire, with larger ones that may have acted as beds on the far side of the house. It was all one big room. Judging from the pots and random cutlery lying around the fireplace, this was the kitchen, living room and bedroom at once.

Lucas appeared by my side and handed me a wooden mug. I sniffed the liquid, but I was thirsty, so I took a sip without asking what I'd been given. The burn of alcohol ran down my throat, followed by sweetness coating my tongue.

The young man grinned. "Asger's secret recipe. You looked like you could use a drink. Now, let's sit down and talk." He took a seat on a fur covered bench, and I joined him, while Asger sat down on the floor opposite. His legs were almost as broad as his tree trunk arms.

I looked at Lucas to compare him to the Viking – and just about managed to suppress a gasp. Lucas only had one arm. One of his shirt sleeves was bound in a knot just below the elbow. A suspicion filtered through my thoughts. The rumour I'd been told after I first met Hjalmar.

"Are you the student?" I asked breathlessly. "The one Hjalmar took into the past and killed?"

Lucas lifted an eyebrow, and I hastily corrected myself. "Not killed, obviously. But you're him?"

He chuckled. "Yes, I'm him. The supposedly dead student. Hjalmar took my arm into the future to prove that I was dead. Glad to know it worked."

I couldn't help but gape at him. "But... why? Everyone thinks Hjalmar is a murderer. Why would you stay here?"

I had to fight back the anger that was trying to bubble to the surface. I was angry on Hjalmar's behalf. Lucas was still alive and if he'd returned to the present, he'd have been able to prove and clear my Viking's reputation.

"Hjalmar?" Asger asked in his deep voice. Poor him, he probably had no idea what we were talking about.

Lucas said something to the Viking in perfect Old Norse. At least it sounded perfect to me. I'd found myself a translator. Great.

"Can you travel back?" I interrupted when they continued talking. "Can you take me back?"

Lucas frowned at me. "Can't you do that yourself?"

I took the broken bracelet out of my pocket. "I can't. And Hjalmar was ripped away from me. We arrived together, in the barn, and then he was gone..."

My voice broke as tears threatened to flow. I was

going to be strong. I was amongst Vikings. I bet none of them ever cried.

"Gone?" Lucas asked sharply. "What do you mean, gone?"

"His bracelet activated without warning and he disappeared before we could do anything. I don't know where he is, or when he's coming back. I'm…"

This time, a tear managed to escape. I quickly wiped it away, but I knew that if I continued to speak, tears would flow for real.

Lucas put a hand – his only hand – on my thigh. "I'm sure he'll be back. He wouldn't leave a student stranded here. Unless it was a test and he wants you to find your own way back?"

I shook my head. "I'm a Hummingbird. I'm not even supposed to time travel, and I have no idea how it's done. And we, well… no, he wouldn't leave me."

I was glad I managed not to blush. I couldn't just tell them that we'd been mostly naked in the barn and that there was no way Hjalmar would have chosen to leave me. Not in that moment. Not when he'd just been about to take me. Make me his.

The knots in my stomach grew tighter. Damn it. I wanted him so much. Needed him. Now that I'd opened my heart for him, it was like a searing wound, bleeding out. He was the only one who could fix it. Mend my heart. How romantic. Urgh.

"Do you know what could have caused this?" I asked when I had my voice under control again.

"Bracelets can malfunction if they're old, but they usually do that while you're in transit. They might spit you out somewhere you didn't intend to go, but I've never heard of one activating just like that. It's very strange."

Asger said something, and I waited for Lucas to translate.

"He says his brother will come for his woman. He's loyal; he'd never abandon the one he loves."

I choked. "His woman? What did you tell him?!"

Lucas chuckled. "Nothing. But we have eyes, you know? It's obvious from the way you blush when you talk about him."

"I didn't blush," I protested.

Asger laughed loudly and pointed at his own cheeks as if he was trying to prove a point. Did he understand some of what we were saying?

This was getting ridiculous. "Tell me why you're here," I demanded and glared at Lucas. "Why didn't you come back? And can you help me return?"

Lucas grew serious, his smile disappearing like the sun behind brooding clouds. "I had to die. It was the only way to live. I'm not going to tell you the whole story, not until I know you can be trusted, but all you need to know is that Hjalmar saved my life. This deception was necessary or I may have been killed in the present. Now I'm a refugee here, trying to live my life as a Viking. Trust me, it's not as romantic as you might think. I miss chocolate. And tea. And coffee. And my computer. And so many other things."

He smiled sadly. "I don't suppose you brought any supplies? He usually brings me some of my favourite foods."

"He did have a bag with him, but that must have disappeared along with him. I'm sorry."

"Oh well, I guess I should be grateful that I have someone to talk to. I never get to speak English anymore. It's a relief to be able to just let the words flow. When I talk to the Norsemen, I have to think about every single word. There are so many ways I could insult someone, and they've barely started accepting me, even though I've been here for two years now."

I gasped. "Two years?"

"Two years, one month and thirteen days. Not that I've been counting." He laughed bitterly. "But I should be grateful that I'm alive. It could have been a lot worse. Asger here has been a great host. He's helped me integrate and learn a trade so that I can support the community. That's made it easier to get people to trust me."

"You're a smith?"

"An apprentice. Asger is the true master smith, I only do the basics to help out. He'd never let me anywhere near his favourite tools."

Asger asked something and Lucas answered in Old Norse, presumably explaining why we'd mentioned his name several times. When Lucas was done, the Viking grinned proudly and got up. He took something from a shelf and handed it to me. It was a tiny metal figurine, only as long as my pinkie. I turned it in my hand, amazed at the detail. I didn't think it was possible to create something so intricate with the tools Vikings had at their disposal. It looked like it could have been 3D-printed, it was that detailed.

"He wants me to translate something word for word," Lucas announced after he'd listened to Asger. "And he wants you to listen without interrupting."

I stared at the Viking in surprise. That sounded very serious.

"Go on," I said before inspecting the figurine some more. It was a woman in a long dress that hugged her body, exposing a thin waist above curvy hips. The dress cut low, showing the edges of her full breasts. Long hair flowed down her back, with a few strands framing her face. Even though the statuette was so small, I could just about make out her features. The woman was young, but not a girl. She had a confidence to her that I wished I possessed.

"Ever since I became a man, I dreamed of a woman," Lucas said, slowly translating Asger's words. I tried to focus on the Viking's words, imagining that I could understand them. "I dream of her most nights. She looks at me, smiles at me, then runs away. I try to follow, I run after her, but I never catch her. Her dress billows behind her, I hear her laughter, her hair flies in the wind, but I never, ever catch up with her."

He paused and I looked at the figurine. "Is that her?"

"Aye. That's her. I always thought that she was just a dream, just part of my imagination. I got used to that thought. I was almost ready to give in to my mum's wishes and marry. Then I saw her. In real life."

I met his eyes, waiting for Lucas to catch up on translating. I was scared of what he was about to say next. I already suspected. I didn't want to hear it.

"The woman I dreamed of is in my house now. She's sitting right in front of me and still, I'm afraid to touch her. I'm scared she might run away like she always does. Will you promise not to run?"

1 A Viking Longhouse

ᚠᚦᛒᛁᛏᚢᚱᛁ 12

To be honest, I was tempted. Get up, leave the house, run away. What was he thinking? Why was he telling me that? He'd already figured out that I was interested in his brother. The decent thing would have been to stay quiet, but instead... Screaming felt like a good option. Or laughing hysterically. I knew the Vikings believed in a lot of things that modern people would consider superstition and magic. Did Asger really think his dreams had been some kind of prophecy? Or was he merely interpreting them as his mysterious dream woman being me?

One thing was clear: I couldn't let him think that I was ready to be *his* woman.

"I'm not going to run," I said, locking eyes with Asger while Lucas translated in the background. "But I'm not the woman from your dream. I'm not going to instantly fall in love with you, move in and have your babies."

Lucas snickered at that, but continued translating.

"I'm only going to be here until Hjalmar returns. Then I'll go back to the present and while I might come back for a visit, or for work, this is not going to be my home. So get it out of your head now."

I took a deep breath, scared of what his reaction might be. He was listening intently, his head cocked to one side. When Lucas finished talking, Asger got up and moved towards me, then knelt down in front of me, so close that his knees touched my feet.

"Are you worried because you already promised to marry my brother?" he asked. "Is that why you're refusing me?"

Lucas started laughing halfway through the sentence and barely managed to convey the message. The Viking growled at him, but that didn't stop Lucas from chuckling. To be fair, it was a bit of a comical situation.

"I have no intentions to marry Hjalmar," I told him, trying very hard not to laugh. "I don't know how it is here, but in my time, women can be with men without marrying them. I only just met Hjalmar and we're still getting to know each other. I'm far too young to marry, and I certainly won't marry Hjalmar just now. So, no, that has nothing to do with it."

Asger smiled. "You don't look too young to marry. Most women have children at your age, but Lucas has told me a lot about your customs. I know you people take it slow."

Lucas snorted again. "I didn't." When Asger glared at him, he straightened his expression and continued with a sigh. "He wants to know if you've been taught about the frille system yet."

I shook my head. "What's that?"

Lucas grimaced. "I don't think I should tell you. This is getting far too personal here. If Asger wants to court you, he can do it himself, without my help. I'm feeling ridiculous. Let's stop talking about love and explore what to do with you."

He was right. I was decidedly uncomfortable talking about all that. I'd only just met these two men, and already Asger was talking about wanting... well, something. I wasn't quite sure what he wanted. Be with me? Keep me here so he could be close to me? Marry me? I didn't like either of those options. The only thing I wanted was to return to my own time. This was an adventure gone wrong.

I got up and handed Asger the little figurine. His eyes turned sad as he looked at me. He'd probably imagined that I'd immediately confess my undying love for him. Well, bad luck.

"I need some air."

I left the hut without looking back.

I was glad that they gave me some time to think. Not that my mind was in any state to come up with a plan of what to do next. My thoughts were full of Hjalmar and Asger, the mystery of Lucas's missing arm and, strangely enough, the Archivist. Not sure what he was doing in my mind. Probably just a side effect of thinking of so many men at once.

I wondered where Hjalmar was now. Back at TTA? Or trapped somewhere in time? For all I knew, he could be in a medieval dungeon or in a spaceship. Trips to the future were forbidden, but everyone knew that the technology to travel back in time also worked to travel forwards. I was sure there was a secret part of the Academy who dealt with the future, but of course, that was just speculation.

Asger was confusing. He seemed like a nice, friendly guy, but he was a little over the top with his dream obsession. I'd have to make it very clear to him that I was not the woman from his dream, and that there was no chance of anything happening between us.

And then there was Lucas, who'd decided to live in the past without anyone in the present knowing that he was still alive. Why would anyone choose to do that? Didn't he have family waiting for him? Mourning his death? There had to be a really good reason, or maybe he was just an incredibly selfish person. Because of him, Hjalmar had been ostracised as a murderer for something he didn't do. Hjalmar had a tough exterior, but I knew that being shunned by everyone had to hurt. It hurt me just thinking about it.

At the same time, I depended on Lucas as a translator and guide. If I was going to have to stay here for a while, I needed him. A full-on confrontation would have to wait.

I really hoped Hjalmar would come back for me soon. This situation was getting ever more complicated. Maybe I should ask if I could stay with Hjalmar's mother? Being around Asger seemed like asking for trouble. I was sure he wasn't just going to give up just because I'd told him that I wasn't interested. He was a Viking, after all. They were known for conquering both land and people.

The door behind me opened, but I didn't turn around. I wanted to make it very clear that my Lainie-needs-alone-time period wasn't over yet. Asger's large body loomed over me, his presence overwhelming.

"Móðir," he said. This time, I actually understood. Mother. He pointed towards a path snaking away from his house. It seemed he wanted to take me to his mother. Hopefully not to tell her that he was going to marry me. I sighed.

"Lucas?" I asked, and he shook his head. Alright then. I was going to follow a Viking who I couldn't converse with to his mother who I wouldn't be able to talk to either. This was getting ridiculous. I wished we'd waited with this time travel excursion until I'd had the time to learn more Old Norse and knowledge about Viking society.

Yesterday, I'd read an article about the role of women in Norse times. It had surprised me how progressive the Vikings seemed in that regard, at least compared to other societies of the same period. Women were allowed to have trades, divorce their husbands – my favourite reason for that was the husband not pleasing the wife in bed – and some of them even fought in battles. Not many, but a few. I wondered if Asger's mother was one of those warrior women.

Asger was already walking away quickly, and I hurried to follow him. The path was a simple line in the dirt, formed by years of people walking along it. Forests loomed all around us in the distance, hiding whatever landscape this village was built in. I wondered if there were fjords for their ships nearby. I really wanted to see a proper Viking ship, ready for the journey across the Atlantic. The Norsemen had travelled all the way down to North Africa, so their boats had to be impressive. Although I wasn't sure what time we'd arrived in. I was going to have to be careful with how much I revealed about my Viking history knowledge – I didn't want to tell them things that hadn't actually happened.

Then I remembered that I wasn't able to communicate with anyone without Lucas, and breathed a sigh of relief. I wasn't going to be able to make a massive mistake like that. Changing the course of history wasn't on my agenda.

Without a backward glance or a single word, Asger led me to the edge of a village. There were about twenty huts, all the same kind of build as his own. In the distance, one larger house loomed above them, much taller and longer than the others. That had to be some kind of community building, or maybe the home of the clan chief?

I really wanted to explore the village, but Asger grunted and pointed at the house closest to us.

"Móðir," he repeated. While his house had been made from bare wood, this one's walls were painted in a reddish hue. Flowers were planted all around it, giving it more of a homely and welcoming feel.

He called out some words before simply walking into the house without knocking on the door. Apprehensively, I followed him. This wasn't just Asger's mother, it was Hjalmar's too. I'm sure my Viking would have introduced us had he got the chance. It was all wrong. It was supposed to be Hjalmar here with me, not Asger. Time was playing a cruel trick on me.

Just like Asger's house, the hut consisted of one large room. Benches covered in animal furs lined the walls closest to us, while a large wooden bed sat at the other end of the hut.

I never got a chance to look around more because a woman launched herself at me, hugging me. This was becoming a tradition. She was smaller than me by at least half a head, but also quite a bit wider. She pressed me against her soft bosom, reminding me of the hugs my grandma had given me before she passed away. She even smelled a bit like my gran. Flowery, warm, friendly.

"It's so good to see you," she said in perfect English, albeit with a slight Nordic accent.

Surprised, I stepped back, leaving her embrace. I couldn't help but stare at her. She was talking English. How the hell...

"I was wondering when Hjalmie would finally bring home a girl. It's taken him long enough. Where is my good-for-nothing son?"

Her wide smile and twinkling eyes immediately made me like her.

"How? Why? Ehm..." I stuttered, words failing me.

She laughed. "He's not told you about me? Oh, that silly boy. I guess the two of you had more important things to talk about... and to do."

She winked at me suggestively, and I felt a blush spread across my cheeks.

Asger started talking in Old Norse, and slowly, the woman's smile began to fade.

"He's disappeared?" she asked, now serious.

I nodded. "There was nothing either of us could do. He was there one second, then gone the next. His bracelet must have malfunctioned."

"Bracelets don't malfunction," she said sharply, before softening her tone. "Someone must have tampered with it. It's possible to program them to automatically activate after a certain time. Usually, that's intended as an emergency tool should the time agent not have a chance to activate the bracelet themselves if they're trapped in a hostile situation. This is highly unusual."

"Excuse me, but how do you know all that?" I asked as politely as I could.

She laughed, but her expression remained worried. "Why, I'm a time agent. I was, anyway, before I fell in love and settled here. Have you never wondered how Hjalmar was allowed to live in the future? Or why he speaks English?"

"I never had the chance," I muttered with a sigh. Everyone seemed to assume that I'd known Hjalmar for much longer than I had. They probably thought I was in my second year or even further along and had time to get to know him. In fact, it had only been a week, although it felt longer.

"Let's sit down and have some tea," the woman said. "I think there's much to discuss."

"Yes," Asger said and I gaped at him. What the fuck?

"You speak English!" I roared at Asger. "Why didn't you say that earlier? Why go through all the charades?"

His mother started to laugh, making her hands shake while she poured us some tea.

"Be gentle on him," she chuckled. "His English is very limited. He refused to learn it as a child, but he understands a lot more than he lets on." She turned to him. "Asger, have you been naughty?"

I couldn't help myself, I snorted. He looked downtrodden, as if he was a boy who was being chastised by his mother.

"Apologise to our guest," she demanded.

"Sorry," he muttered, not meeting my eyes. "I sorry."

"I *am* sorry," his mother corrected. "I wish you hadn't been so stubborn when you were a boy. Knowing a second language can be so helpful."

Asger grumbled something into his beard. I was no longer trying to hide my grin. This was gold. Seeing him put down by his mother... I was loving it.

"I'm Lainie," I said after taking a sip of tea, realising that we'd never been introduced to each other.

The woman smiled at me and held out a hand. "Heather."

We shook hands, which was a little weird since we'd already hugged.

"So, you're from my time?" I asked after a moment's hesitation.

She nodded. "What year did you come from?"

"Twenty-one thirteen."

"You're two decades after me then, although I've been here for much longer than that. I met my husband when I was in my late twenties and when Hjalmar came along... Time travel when pregnant is not advisable, and young children can't travel either, so we decided to settle down. I got so involved in this society that I never went back to my job. This has become my home."

"Do you ever miss the present? Your past, I mean? No, is it your future?"

She chuckled at my confusion. "To be honest, not in the slightest. Things here are so much more honest. People say what they mean. Their religion and sense of honour keep them in line. If someone here promises you something, they will do it, no matter what. A Viking would rather die than break an oath."

"Vikings strong," Asger said with a proud grin. "Fight women."

Heather laughed. "I think you mean fight *for* women. Or fighting women." She turned to me. "I've always thought Asger would fall for a warrior woman, but so far, he's sticking to his silly idea of finding the woman from his dreams."

I cringed as Asger started jabbering in Old Norse,

gesticulating towards me. Heather's eyes widened as she listened to him.

"Has he told you?" she asked when her son had finished.

I nodded, not able to hide a grimace. "He has indeed. And I've told him that I'm not interested."

Asger started talking again, but his mother cut him off. She quickly said something to him, then translated for me. "I told him that it's your decision. I've always taught him to respect women, and he's not going to stop now. If he gets too much for you, let me know, and I'll knock some sense into him."

From the glare she gave her son, I could imagine that her talking-to would be rather effective. Having raised two Viking boys, Heather had to be formidable and used to making them do what she wanted. I liked her more and more.

"Frille," Asger said, a defiant look appearing on his face. "Tell she."

Heather sighed. "Seriously?"

"Tell," Asger repeated, more forcefully this time.

"I'm not sure I want to hear this," I muttered, remembering how Lucas had refused to explain about whatever frille was.

"Tell."

"I don't think he's going to let it go," Heather said, exasperation lacing her tone. "I'll tell you but just because he won't shut up otherwise. The frille system allows Viking men to take several wives. Mistresses, if you wish. Most clan chiefs do it for political reasons, to ally with as many other clans and important families as possible. There's nothing immoral or dishonourable about being a frille, and some women aspire to be one.

You share the work of dealing with a man with other women, and if you get fed up of him, you can always divorce him." She laughed. "Sometimes I wished I had a sister-wife who could help me when my husband was behaving like an idiot. An extra pair of hands would have been handy in the household as well."

"You mentioned divorce," I said slowly. "What happens after though? Would other men not look down at a woman who's been a mistress?"

Heather shook her head. "Not at all. Some women become a frille, give their husband a child, all for political reasons, then divorce him and marry the man they actually love. The system has its benefits, although I personally was glad that my husband didn't take any frille. Nor sex slaves, but that's an entirely different matter."

I shuddered at the thought of slaves. I knew it was normal in Viking society, but everything within me rebelled against that. It didn't agree with my morals.

I mulled it over. "Why does he want me to know about frille, though?" I asked Heather. "He's not married, is he? Or does he want to marry me and then take on other wives?"

Outrage bubbled up in me. Even though I wasn't interested in him, I also felt a little betrayed and jealous when thinking about sharing him. Not that I wanted him. It shouldn't matter. I should just finish this conversation and find out how I was going to find Hjalmar.

"I think he's trying to tell you that he'd be alright to share. That he could be your frille, even if you're with Hjalmar."

Asger nodded. I couldn't help but stare at him. He wanted to share me? With his brother? That was fucking disturbing.

It was, right? Then why was there heat pooling in my stomach and why was my heart beating faster?

"Is that normal?" I asked slowly. "One woman having several husbands?"

Heather shook her head. "Not officially. Adultery is a crime, although a woman isn't expected to be a virgin when she marries and she can be with men before committing to marriage. So I guess in theory, you could have multiple lovers if you don't marry one of them."

Asger grunted something, and his mother nodded. "But we're talking as if you were bound by Viking laws. You're not. You're an outsider, which pretty much means that you can make your own rules. That's what I did whenever I wanted to do something that's not proper in their eyes. I'd simply say that we did things like that back where I came from. They're pretty accepting of that. So if you told them it's normal to have several husbands in your country, then that would work."

I sat down my teacup and got up. "Well, I'm not going to do that. I'm not interested. All I want is find Hjalmar and be with him."

Asger grunted in annoyance and got up as well. He blocked my way to the door, towering over me. He was so broad that I couldn't even see the door.

"Let me go," I demanded.

"No." He looked down at me, his eyes boring into mine. They were a shade lighter than his brother's, but just as stunning. "You mine."

"Listen, you caveman, I'm not yours nor am I anybody else's. I decide what I want to do, and right now, I want to go outside and get some air."

Heather snorted, but Asger didn't move.

"Mine," he growled and put his hands on my shoulders. A strange warmth shot through me at his touch and I froze. That warmth... it felt familiar, somehow. Like it was meeting an ache I hadn't realised as there. My body relaxed without my doing and suddenly, I was in his arms. He pressed me against his chest, adding more of the warmth. It was flowing through my entire body, making my gooseflesh rise and a pleasant shiver run down my back. Instinctively, I leaned against him, returning the hug, increasing our connection. He didn't try to kiss me or turn it into anything more than an embrace. He simply held me. He probably knew that I would have pushed him away had he tried something else. But this I could handle. I needed that warmth, that heat that was slowly pooling in my chest. I'd never felt anything like it. It was both beautiful and scary at once.

I heard Heather move away, giving us space, but I didn't care. All that mattered was his touch. The way our bodies fit together like pieces of a puzzle. My softness met his hardness. I didn't want to feel what I did, but I couldn't resist the pull. I wanted him. My mind was going crazy, shouting at me that I wasn't the kind to jump guys, that I'd only just met him, that we'd never even properly talked - but it meant nothing. My body as pressed against his and the effect of the close embrace was beginning to show. His erection pressed against my belly and my nipples were hard against his chest. What the hell was I doing?

No. I was with Hjalmar. Or at least I was going to be, once I found him again. I was confusing the two men. They were brothers, so similar. That had to be it. With one enormous effort, I stepped back, pushing him away.

The heartbreak in his eyes almost made me hug him

again. I looked down at the floor, refusing to meet his gaze.

"I'll be outside," I muttered and ran around him and out of the door before he could stop me.

ONCE AGAIN, I was outside a Viking hut, unable to sort out my thoughts. I sat down on a narrow bench and closed my eyes, listening to the distant sounds of the village. There were very few people around, but it still afternoon, so I assumed most people were working. Raiding distant lands wasn't the only thing they did. By the time the sunset, there were probably going to be more people around.

Inside, Heather was talking to Asger in Old Norse, but even if I had spoken the language, their voices were too quiet to make out. I hope she was trying to discourage him from his weird frille notion. Right now, all I was interested in was finding Hjalmar. Once he'd returned, I'd focus on going home, although I might question Lucas first about why he was pretending to be dead. Maybe there was a chance of restoring Hjalmar's reputation. I didn't want him to stay the outcast he was, although somehow, I was pretty sure it was by his own choosing. He wasn't a crowd pleaser, not in the slightest. Well, I was the same. In the week I'd spent at the Academy, the only people I'd really talked to were Maryam and Kaycee. Maryam had become something of a friend, and Kaycee... someone I really didn't like but who I was just about able to be around. I didn't think she'd make it at TTA for long, not the way she kept annoying teachers by being entitled and not doing her homework.

A random thought – what if I never saw them again – burst into my mind, but I pushed it away as quickly as it had arrived. This wasn't the time to get melancholic. It was time to act. There were two other people here who had time travel experience. Lucas was only a student, but Heather was a trained time agent. Together, we might have a chance.

I sighed. I didn't want to go back inside, especially not now that they'd started shouting at each other. It was mostly Asger doing the shouting. I felt bad for Heather, but she knew how to handle herself. She'd brought up two Vikings; she had to be able to deal with their tantrums.

The shouting stopped, and a moment later, Heather stepped outside. Without a word, she sat down on the bank beside me. I was half expecting Asger to storm out of the hut as well, but he stayed inside.

"My sons can be selfish sometimes," Heather said with a smile. "They got it from their father. Hjalmar brought you here against his better knowledge, and now Asger is trying to prevent me from giving you this."

She pulled something from a linen bag slung across her shoulder. It looked far too advanced to be of Viking origins. She turned the object in her hands and a strange expression flickered across her face.

"Those bracers have evolved a lot since I was a time agent," she said quietly, then handed it to me. "Doesn't this one look clunky in comparison?"

I took a closer look, recognising some of the same markings that had covered my own bracelet. This one, however, was massive, large enough to cover the entire lower arm. There was a hole for the thumb as well, so it had to reach all the way up to the back of the hand. If that was what time travel bracelets had looked like in the past, they really had changed a lot since then. The one Hjalmar had put around my wrist had been elegant, looking almost like jewellery. This was the opposite of elegant.

Heather pulled a second bracer from her bag. "I was given these when I told my boss that I was going to live in the past. Back then, I still planned to return after Hjalmar was older, but then Asger came along, and by the time both of them were old enough for me to leave for several weeks at a time, I'd got used to my simple life. I didn't want to be a time agent any longer. Still, I kept the bracers. I'd been given two in case me or my husband fell ill and needed modern treatment. Sadly, I never got the chance to use it. My husband died instantly, a heart attack. No time to take him to the future."

She sighed, her thumbs rubbing the metal of her bracer.

"I'm sorry," I whispered, and she turned and smiled at me, her eyes full of sadness.

"It was hard. Whenever a child got sick in the village, or when the men came back from battle with missing limbs and searing wounds, I was tempted to take them into the future, use those bracelets to save their lives. But I had taken an oath to only use them for my own family, so I kept them hidden, never telling anyone about them. Until Hjalmar turned of age and decided he wanted to see where his mother had come from. I took him to the Academy, and he stayed there, getting the same training I had when I was his age."

"And you returned back here?"

She nodded. "Yes, I couldn't stay away from Asger and my husband. They needed me more than Hjalmar did. He's always been the more independent of the two. But it was hard not to see Hjalmar for three years. Still, I'd promised that I'd only use the bracers in an emergency. Now, I think this qualifies as one."

I gaped at her. "You can take me back?"

Heather smiled. "You were never trapped. Sorry if you thought that. Together with Lucas's bracelet, we have three at our disposal. I don't think he's going to be able to join you though. It would be far too dangerous for him."

"I don't know how to programme them," I admitted. "I've only been at the Academy for a week, I wouldn't have been allowed to time travel for years had Hjalmar not taken me here."

She chuckled. "He's always liked to break rules. I only saw his TTA reports after he graduated, but let me tell you, they were quite the read. I think he committed every single offence that was possible without getting expelled. I'm not surprised in the slightest that he would inspire someone else to break the rules along with him."

"Can we go now?" I asked quickly, too impatient to listen to what I'm sure are very amusing stories. We could do that once I was back in his arms.

"Not quite, I need to sync these old bracers with Lucas's modern one. They should be compatible, but it may take some time for me to figure it out."

"Why do we need all three? Isn't it enough if the two of us travel together?"

She sighed deeply. "I promised Asger that he could come along. It was his condition in return for giving me the keys to the bracers. I should never have given it to him, but we were worried that people might come after Lucas, and Asger is far better suited to protect both our guest and the bracers."

"Asger? But he doesn't speak any English! He'll stick out like a sore thumb!"

The words broke out of me before I could stop myself, before I could consider that I was talking about her son.

A frown joined her smile. "I know you're feeling overwhelmed by him just now, but he only has your and his brother's best interests at heart. We don't know who tampered with Hjalmar's bracelet or why they did it. He might be in danger, and Asger is a strong warrior. He'll be good to have on our side."

She was right, but that didn't mean I had to like it. I could still feel that strange warmth inside of me from when he'd hugged me. I didn't want to crave more of it, but I did. I wanted to be in his arms again and hated my stupid emotions for desiring that.

"I hope to get it sorted by tomorrow," Heather promised. "I assume you'd rather stay with me than with the boys?"

I laughed. "You bet."

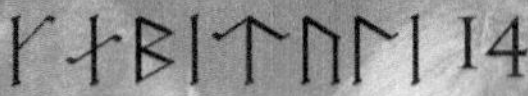

CHAPTER 14

We're on a boat with nothing but tall waves all around us. The boat rocks from side to side and foam sprinkles my face, but I don't feel scared.

There's someone else in the boat behind me, I feel his comforting presence, but I don't want to turn around to look at him. He's a friend, someone I know very well. He steers the boat with an expert touch, avoiding the biggest waves that could easily crush our little boat. I feel safe with him, even though I can't see his face.

"The storm will pass," he says confidently. "The sea will guide us where we need to be."

I nod, taking his words as the truth.

"I'm glad you decided to come out with me today. It gets lonely sometimes."

I nod again. I don't remember getting on this boat with him, but I don't feel like I need to have that memory. It doesn't matter. The past doesn't matter, nor does the future. The present is what's important.

There's a massive wave coming towards us, taller than several houses stacked upon each other.

"It's going to drown us!" I shout when the boat continues to steer towards us.

"No," the man behind me says calmly. "Don't be scared. Nothing bad will happen."

I trust him, but I can't help but clench my fists as the wave approaches. It's getting ever bigger, foam glistening on its curved top.

When it hits us, our boat glides into the water, taking us down into the depths of the sea. I can breathe underwater and I don't question it. The boat continues its journey as if we were still on the surface of the ocean. Deeper and deeper we go, the light of the sun dimming until we're in a gloomy underwater world.

Glowing fish swim all around us, illuminating the darkness.

The sea floor becomes a road for our boat, guiding us as the man behind us steers us to an unknown destination.

Suddenly, a dark shadow appears on our right, a shape so massive that it could be a hill if it weren't moving.

"Jǫrmungandr," the man whispers. In awe-stricken silence, we approach the body of the serpent that's stretched out across the bottom of the sea. There is no end to it; a mountain of scales and rippling muscle.

SEPARATED BY TIME, UNITED IN DREAM.

The voice of the serpent echoes in my mind and I bow my head in reverence. This is the World Serpent, the child of the God Loki, the being that surrounds Midgard, grasping its own tail within its jaws. The day it unfurls, Ragnarök will begin.

The boat approaches the serpent's head, and with relief I see that it's still biting its tail in its giant jaws. The end of the world hasn't begun yet.

SO MANY TIMES YOU HAVE BEEN HERE, YET NO TIMES AT ALL.

None of what Jǫrmungandr says makes sense, but I listen nonetheless, knowing that this being is wise and nearly omniscient. Even if I don't understand its words now, they might reveal their true meaning in the future.

YOU'RE BOUND TO EACH OTHER, YET YOU STAY APART, WAITING FOR THE MOMENT THAT WILL EXPOSE YOUR SOULS.

I know he's talking about me and the man behind me. I've still not turned around. Something is stopping me from looking at him.

CHILDREN OF TIME. YOU NO LONGER HAVE TO WAIT.

The man gasps but doesn't say anything.

I SHALL RETURN YOUR MEMORIES TO YOU THAT YOU GAVE TO ME FOR SAFE KEEPING.

I did that? I can't remember. I've never been here before. Never met Jǫrmungandr. I would remember its greatness.

"What memories?" I ask quietly.

THE MEMORIES OF YOUR SHARED FUTURE. USE THEM WELL. IF YOU DON'T, THAT FUTURE MIGHT NEVER COME TO PASS AND THE CIRCLE WILL BE BROKEN.

A flash of light.

Sunlight.

We're running over a field of green grass and dandelions, our feet naked, our clothes fluttering in a gentle breeze. I laugh at the sheer joy of the moment.

He is behind me, following me. We're running towards our favourite spot at the top of the cliff. I'm faster than him, but he tries to race me nonetheless.

"Slow down!" he shouts, but I continue running. My feet barely touch the ground as I speed towards the cliff. My clothes feel too tight as I think of what he's going to do to me

once we reach it. It's where we go when we need some alone time.

I grin as he keeps shouting for me to stop. He's a sore loser. I don't know why he insists on racing me. He loses every single time. Luckily, he's got enough stamina to satisfy me after, even though he'll be out of breath.

I reach the top of the cliff long before he arrives, panting, his cheeks red behind his blond beard. I love how his beard feels when we kiss. It's softer than it looks and it adds to the already thrilling sensation of having his lips on mine.

"You're so slow," I tease him.

"You run like the Valkyries of Valhalla," he groans, clutching his sides. "Are you sure you're human?"

"Valkyries have wings. Why would they run?" I quip, eliciting a breathless laugh.

"You're getting too cocky," Asger huffs.

I blink at him, all innocence. "You're the one with the cock."

He meets my eyes, burning with desire. I grin and slide my dress over my shoulders at the same time as he takes off his shirt. His chest is covered in scars, and I know each and every one of them. They each tell a story. Some of those he has told me, others he has kept for future times. Some stories he will likely never tell. He's been through wars, he's seen things that he'd rather forget.

He takes off his linen trousers, stepping out of them easily since his feet are as bare as mine. He grins at me, his expression turning into that of a predator. I'm his willing prey.

Asger stalks towards me until we're just a breath apart.

"On your knees," he says hoarsely, and I follow his command without question. I love it when he takes charge.

His cock is hard already, ready for me. His one remaining ball is waiting for my attention. I smile and run my tongue along his length, marking him as mine. He's mine through and through. My Viking.

Asger groans when I reach the end of his shaft. He puts his hands around my head, entangling his fingers in my long silky hair. He pushes me closer to his cock, but I fight him a little.

"What's my prize today?" I ask, stalling for time. Not because I don't want to suck his cock, but because I want to increase the anticipation for both of us. It will make it even better.

"You're greedy, you know that?"

I chuckle and teasingly swipe my tongue against his head, licking up a pearl of pre-cum.

"It was your idea to race," I reply with a grin. His taste fills my mouth, and I can barely stop myself from taking him all the way into my mouth.

Asger sighs. "A truth. You get to ask a question and I will tell you the truth, the whole truth. So I swear."

"You're dramatic, you know that?"

He laughs. "Ask your question before I change my mind, little Valkyrie."

My mind is blank. It's an opportunity to find out more about my lover, but all I can think about is how much my body craves him. How much I want to taste him. Feel him inside me. Come at the same time as him.

My gaze falls on his cock and what waits at the other end.

"How did you lose your other ball?"

He sucks in a sharp breath. I've asked that question before, but he never answered. Now, he has to. He gave me his word, the most precious thing any Viking possesses. I almost feel bad for it, but I won this truth fair and square. I would have been happy with another prize.

"Fuck me," he says roughly and takes his hands from my head. "Ride me, clench your cunt around my cock, let me hold *your swollen breasts as they whip up and down, and then I will tell you.*

My body burns with heat at his words, the same intense warmth that I always feel in his presence. He lies on the grass and I lower myself onto him until the tip of his cock presses against my entrance.

"You don't have to tell me," I say quietly when his intense blue eyes capture mine. "We can fuck without your secrets."

He shakes his head. "I gave you my word. I was planning to tell you anyway, at some point."

Suddenly he grabs my hips and pushes me down, impaling me on his cock. I'm used to his girth, but it's still a surprise every time that I can somehow take him. I moan when he starts to move in me, rocking his hips up again and again. He wanted me to ride him, but for now, he's the active one, thrusting into me with all the strength of a Viking warrior.

"Our village was attacked once," he says without stopping his thrusts. "We were unprepared and most of the men were at sea. I managed to get most of the villagers into the longhouse, which had the strongest walls. We thought it would be easiest to defend. The other men were patrolling outside, and I was guarding the door from the inside. We'd barred the door, thinking that the men outside were enough to defend us. I heard them die."

He thrusts into me with new fervour, his fingernails burrowing into my hips. I match his pace, grinding against him, riding him like he wanted me to.

"One by one, they died. Then they started knocking against the door. I was ready to defend my people, my village, but I knew I had no chance of succeeding. I was one against many. They threatened to burn down the longhouse, burn us all alive, but their chief was having a good day. He offered us a bargain. Our lives in return for my humiliation. I was inside

the house with the women and children. He said he wanted me to turn into a woman too, as proof of my cowardice. He thought I'd been hiding with them, even though I was there to defend my friends, my family."

He's fucking me like he never has before, ramming into me without pause. The pain is evident in his entire body. He's reliving the memory, and the only way he can cling onto the present is by being with me, in me. I wish there was more I could do, but I know I can't interrupt him now. He needs to finish his story. I give him my body as an anchor, a lifeline that he can cling to.

"They hacked a hole into the door, not to get in, but to watch. To watch me cut off my own balls. I took my axe, the axe that had killed many men before, and put it to my crotch. But I didn't want to spoil my axe with my own blood, so I asked one of the women for a knife. A sharp one. I wrapped a hand around my balls, telling myself that this was a small price to pay for the lives of my people. Outside, they were jeering, while their chief was watching me with a grin on his face. I stared him down, looked at him as I sliced through my flesh.

"He laughed when I held up my ball as proof, then told me to cut off the second one. That's when I heard shouts in the backgrounds. The others were returning! Before the chief could react, I threw the knife at him. It flew through the hole in the door as if Óðinn himself was guiding my hand, embedding itself in the man's eye. He was dead, and the shock and surprise of his kinsmen were enough to distract them. They never realised that the rest of our warriors had returned just at the right moment. We prevailed, although the cost was great."

He stops his thrusts for a moment, making me realise how much I'm hurting. Not just my body, my heart. For him.

"You're more of a man than others who still have both balls," I whisper, gently touching his cheek.

"I'm not talking about my balls. It was a small price to pay. No, I lost friends that day. They're now waiting for me in the halls of Valhalla. While I was healing, fighting the weakness that overcame me again and again, I often wished to join them. But not anymore."

His eyes continue his story. Because of you, *they say.*

I bend forward and kiss him, bruising his lips like he's bruised my body.

"You're the bravest man I know," I whisper in between kisses.

And then I sit up and grind my hips, faster and faster, showing him how much I care for him. Together, we soar, our bodies moving as one, coming undone at the same moment.

At the beginning, when I first saw him naked, he thought that I might think less of him. That I might not want him.

He couldn't have been more wrong.

ᚠᚨᛒᛁᛏᚢᚱ 15

I ran through the night, trying to find my way back to Asger's house. I needed to know. Needed to *see*. I'd woken up covered in sweat and wet between my legs. Like I'd actually been with the Viking.

The dream had been so real, unlike anything I'd ever experienced before. Not so much the thing about the sea serpent, but the bit after. The sex. This hadn't just been a wet dream. It had been so much more than that.

Dawn was slowly turning the darkness into shades of grey, exposing the silhouette of Asger's hut in the distance. Smoke was rising from the hole in the roof, signalling me to come closer.

Before I reached the house, the door banged open, and a large figure stepped outside.

I didn't hesitate. I flung myself at him, right into his wide open arms. There was no question about it. He'd had the same dream. While I was wearing a long cotton shirt that Heather had given me, Asger was naked. His arousal pressed against me as he held me in his arms.

I couldn't help it. I pushed him away a little and

looked down. Damn. It was too dark to see any details. I took his hand and wordlessly pulled him closer to his hut, where the shine of a fire illuminated the grass around the door.

He let me turn him towards the light, his expression hopeful. He wanted me to see it. To believe that it hadn't been a dream.

I looked at his cock. Only one ball was dangling behind his very hardened manhood.

"Fuck," I muttered, completely thrown off guard even though I had kind of expected this.

Something strange was happening. Something that I couldn't explain. I'd seen us together and I'd known that we were in a relationship and had been for a while. I saw us make out at the top of a cliff, like we had many times before. Did I really see the future? Did he? Or did I simply read something into a dream?

"Fuck?" Asger asked with a grin. "Fuck?"

He pulled me close again, his cock rubbing against my belly. Damn, that felt good. And familiar. Then I remembered that I'd technically never been with a man, and put a hand on his chest, pushing him away.

"Not now," I whispered hoarsely. I wanted him; my body was screaming for him. But no, I couldn't let the future determine the present. If that had been the future. I wished Hjalmar was here to help me figure it out. I could talk to Heather, but did I really want to tell her that I'd slept with her son in a dream and now wanted to feel him inside me again? And again... and again... until I was raw and sore and satisfied.

"Soon?" he asked, his voice gleaming with hope.

I sighed. "Maybe. I need to figure this out in my head.

Let's go and find Hjalmar first, and then we can see. Okay?"

I realised he probably didn't understand what I'd just said. In the dream, he'd spoken perfect English, albeit with an accent. Did that make it more likely that it had just been my imagination? But how would I have known about the missing testicle? I'd never seen him naked, and Hjalmar hadn't told me anything about his brother. Something strange was going on here.

I stepped around him and walked into the hut.

"Lucas!" I shouted, my eyes having trouble to adjust to the light. "I need you!"

Movement at the back of the house made me walk that way. Two beds lined the back wall, one for each of the men. Lucas stumbled towards me, his hair messy, his eyes half-shut.

"Whatsamatter?"

He yawned loudly and rubbed his eyes.

"Translate for us," I ordered, not caring that I was being rude. "Ask Asger what he dreamed. Why he came running out to meet me."

"Huh?"

"Do it," I said impatiently.

Lucas sighed. "I have no idea what's going on, but alright, if you let me sleep again after." He turned to Asger and started talking to him in Old Norse. "He says he had the same dream he always has. A woman running away from him. This time though, he didn't wake up before he could catch up with her. This time, he..."

Lucas blushed when Asger kept talking. "He... ehm... he made love to her."

I snorted. "Is that what he said? Made love?"

The young man cringed. "No. His words were a little

cruder. Very crude. Not something I need to repeat, or even imagine. Anyway, he says they... made love... and that he told her a story. How he lost his precious stones-"

He gaped at me. "Wait, he actually told that woman? I've been pestering him ever since I arrived here, and he's always refused to talk about it."

I shrugged. "Maybe he didn't want to talk about it to another man?"

"It still isn't fair," Lucas muttered. "I was here first."

"Maybe you should have tried sleeping with him," I quipped. Asger started laughing. I needed to figure out how much English he actually understood. Was he just toying with me? Did he comprehend every word I said? If he did... he was dead.

"I tried." Lucas chuckled. "Turns out Asger isn't into men. Such a pity. He's totally my type."

"You're gay?" I asked, a little surprised.

"Pansexual. I love who I love, irrespective of gender. I do have a thing for Vikings though. There's that one guy in the village... well, he's so hot he'd turn any straight man gay. That kind of hot." He licked his lips. "Asger has suggested I should become the guy's sex slave. That's the only way I could be with him. He's married and while he could take female frille, he could only have a man as his slave. Stupid rules."

Asger said something and Lucas groaned. "Yes, Vikings don't like to submit, and being penetrated by another man counts as submission. If you do that, you basically become worthless in everyone's eyes. Much easier to be a slave who can't complain. No one would tell a slave that he's doing something wrong if his master is sleeping with him."

It was fascinating, but how did we end up talking

about gay Viking sex? I had something more important on my mind. Sorry, gay Vikings. I wasn't homophobic, just busy.

"Ask him what he thinks this means. I need to know."

Lucas nodded and translated my question for Asger, who immediately started talking quickly, waving his hands around in emphasis. How I wished that I could understand him. My basic Old Norse knowledge was useless here. How had I ever thought I'd be able to communicate with the locals?

"Asger thinks it's a side effect of time travel. He says his mother had visions of her husband before they ever met. Time isn't linear, it's not a straight string you travel along. Sometimes, the string curls and touches a part of the past or future, giving us a rare glimpse into what might happen."

"Might?" I asked sharply.

"Time isn't reliable. Things change all the time. A tiny pebble that you throw off a mountain could create an avalanche, wiping out a village, preventing someone important from every being born. Wars could be fought that would never have existed. Every action has consequences, no matter how small. That's why the TTA was founded. To help us prevent from setting off a ripple effect when we travel in time."

I blushed. "We never got to that part," I muttered.

"Well, let's get you back so that you can go back to your lessons," Lucas said, not unkindly. "But first, I need some more sleep. We all do. Tired time travel is best avoided. You need a clear head."

I huffed. Even with some more sleep, my head wouldn't be any clearer. A certain Viking had barricaded himself in my mind and was doing his best to remind me of his presence, no matter what I did.

WE ASSEMBLED in front of Asger's house. It was further away from the village than Heather's hut, and we didn't want to be seen. I hadn't found out yet where the Vikings thought Lucas had come from, but we certainly didn't want any of them to see three of us disappear into thin air.

Heather handed Asger and me a bracer each, while she took the more modern one that Lucas had given her. The young man was standing a little removed from us, watching with sadness in his eyes.

I walked towards him while Asger was talking to his mother.

"Are you alright?" I asked. "Are you sure you don't want to come?"

Lucas looked at me, and I realised it wasn't just sadness mirroring in his expression. There was fear mixed into it, a deep-rooted angst that made me understand why he was here. Why he wasn't in the present.

"If anyone sees me there, I'll be dead," he said quietly. "I only survived thanks to Hjalmar. I don't think I'll ever be able to return." He shrugged and looked around. The sun was slowly making its way across the sky, reflecting on dew drops on the grass around our feet. The smell of smoke filled the air, the result of fire being the Vikings' only source of light and warmth. I doubt I would ever get the smoke out of my uniform. I was wearing it again, while Asger was in a strange sort of suit that looked like it had been modelled on modern fashion, but executed with the wrong materials and techniques. Heather wore a dress that was timeless enough not to stand out in either society.

Lucas handed me a folded piece of paper. It was notepaper, just like the one I'd used at the Academy. "It's a shopping list," he said with a sheepish grin. "All the things I miss most. Could you give it to Hjalmar, once you find him? Or bring those items here yourself? Even if they don't let you travel again until you're done with your training, it will only be mere days for me if you travel to this same time destination. I can spend a few days without chocolate."

His smile turned sad. "I hope you'll find Hjalmar. He's a good friend. A good man."

"We need to go!" Heather shouted from behind me. "I don't know how long I can keep up the flow of energy between the bracers. Hurry!"

I rushed to her and held my arm against hers. Asger touched his bracer to mine, and without warning, both of them began to vibrate. My entire arm was shaking. This was very different from the bracelet that had brought me here.

"What was the date when you left?" Heather asked impatiently. I told her and she keyed in something into the holographic display of her bracelet. I felt Lucas watching us from afar, but I didn't turn to look at him. I couldn't get distracted. This was our only chance to return, to find Hjalmar.

"You need to focus on the present as hard as you can," Heather instructed. "You're the one with the strongest link. Asger has never been there, and the last time I was at the Academy was when Hjalmar graduated. You're our anchor, the only way we can find the right time. Now hold hands."

I did as she asked. We stood in a triangle, our hands entwined, the bracers vibrating like crazy.

Lucas started shouting something in Old Norse, likely aimed at Asger, but then we were ripped apart, our stomachs pulled from our bodies, our minds driven from our heads. It was torture, the worst pain I'd ever felt. My body was disintegrating, being torn in all directions, in all times.

"Concentrate!"

I barely heard Heather's shout, but it was enough to make me focus on Hjalmar. The pain was worth it if we managed to get to him. He was worth the pain.

Asger screamed close to my ear, his voice so similar to that of his brother, but not quite the same. I hoped he wasn't feeling the same pain I was.

On and on it went. Flickers of images flew across my mind, too fast to make out any details. Was I seeing time? My own past? Someone else's?

Then it was over. No warning. No crash landing.

I was kneeling on the ground, two polished shoes in front of me. The stone floor looked familiar, but it was moving somehow, like waves on the sea. My body didn't feel right. Like I hadn't quite arrived in the present yet. I looked up, barely making out the familiar figure of the Archivist, before bending over and puking all over his feet.

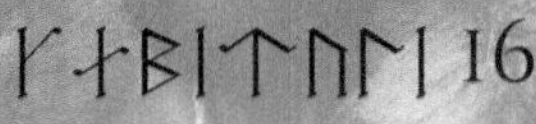

CHAPTER 16

The Archivist led us through the secret passage, away from the hustle and bustle of the Academy. Above us, students were going about their business, unaware that there was a Viking and his mother in the building. Asger's expression was one of wonder, his eyes wide, his lips slightly parted as he took in our surroundings. We'd not even seen any computers or technology, yet he was already amazed.

Heather didn't seem fazed by being back after such a long time, but she was smiling as we hurried down the stairs and towards the Archive. I wonder how much time had passed since Hjalmar and I disappeared. Hjalmar had promised me that it would only be mere minutes, but that was before he went missing and we had to rely on old-time travel tech. At least the Archivist had recognised me, which meant we hadn't returned before I'd met him. He was muttering to himself, probably about having to clean his shoes. Oops. Based on my time travel performance just now, I wouldn't have made it into the fast track stream. My stomach still felt queasy.

He hadn't deigned us with any words besides 'follow me', so when he stayed quiet, I couldn't hold it back any longer.

"When are we?" I asked.

He didn't reply, but the tension in his shoulders increased. Something was going on, something that went beyond me puking on him.

When we entered the archive, he looked around warily, checking if anyone else was around. Luckily, we were alone. He led us in a small back room adjacent to his office. Two battered leather sofas lined the walls, but together with some dusty bookshelves, they were the only furniture.

"Is there a bathroom down here?" I dared to ask. I really wanted to clean up my face and wash out my mouth.

"Straight ahead, a small door on the right next to the entrance to the secret passage."

I nodded my thanks and hurried away to make myself feel a little more human. Not just because I felt disgusting, but also because I had the urge to present myself in the best light to Asger. And the Archivist. And Hjalmar, once we found him again. My heart was splitting itself in three, even though that was completely idiotic and selfish. Besides, the Archivist hadn't shown any interest in me. I was simply interested in him because he was so mysterious. I didn't like secrets and mysteries, that's what it was. Nothing else.

The bathroom looked like it hadn't been used in decades, but at least the tap worked. I threw some water on my face and washed out my mouth, then rubbed some water into the worst stains on my uniform. I was going to murder whoever had decided to make our jumpsuits white. It was entirely impractical.

I gave up when I seemed to only make it worse, smudging the dirt to places that had previously been almost clean. Once I found out what was going on, I'd be able to go up to my room and change. And shower.

When I returned, Heather and the Archivist were talking animatedly, while Asger sat on a sofa by himself, staring at the tablet the Archivist was holding in his hand. I wonder what he saw it as. Witchcraft? Or had his mother prepared him for this by telling him what kind of tech we had in the future? He looked entirely out of his depth. I sat by his side and put a hand on his thigh.

He looked at me in surprise, then put his hand on mine and squeezed. The tension in the way he held himself decreased a little, but he still seemed uncomfortable.

"What are they accusing him of?" Heather asked the Archivist, and I stared at her, wishing I'd heard the full conversation. Was she talking about Hjalmar?

"Murder. Obstructing the course of justice. Kidnapping. Plus a few other, even more ridiculous things. I don't know how anyone could believe he did any of those. I barely know him and yet I doubt he'd be able to do even one of those. He's an honourable man."

Heather nodded. "That he is. He may have a rebellious streak, but I raised him to stick to the law, Viking or modern. He always had a disadvantage back home as the son of a stranger, a woman who appeared out of nowhere, so I didn't want to give them an excuse to turn him into a scapegoat."

"Wait, what's going on?" I blurted. "Is Hjalmar here?"

The Archivist turned to me, his expression grave. "He's been imprisoned for the past two weeks."

"Two weeks?" I interrupted. "I've been gone for two weeks?"

He nodded, then glared at me. "What were you thinking? A first-year student travelling in time? Without experience, without permission?"

I blushed. "I had Hjalmar with me. He's a teacher, so it wasn't like I did it by myself."

He pointed at my hand; his eyes cold. "I thought I could trust you, instead, it turns out you're the thief. You pretended to be all innocent and trustworthy, yet you'd broken into my Archive to steal that ring. Was it fun, playing me? Did it make you feel good?"

I gaped at him. "You believe I stole the ring?"

I ripped it off my finger and threw it at him. "Have it. I didn't take it, I didn't play you, I never pretended to be anything I'm not. But if you believe that, I guess that tells me everything I need to know about you."

Anger ran through my veins and I was tempted to jump up and storm out of the room. Asger squeezed my hand and I looked at him.

"Hjalmar," he said simply. "Hjalmar."

I nodded and fought the rage I felt towards the Archivist. Asger was right, this wasn't about the Archivist and me, it was about Hjalmar and how we could help him.

"Where are they holding him?" Heather asked in her soft voice.

The Archivist gave me one more glare, then turned back to her. "I'm not sure. He could be here at the Academy, or in the Time Agency Headquarters. It depends how dangerous they think him to be. I believe Headmistress Tape has vouched for him, but in the end, it's not her decision."

"I can't believe they hacked his bracelet," Heather muttered. "It's against the law."

He laughed harshly. "A lot of things are against the law, but recently, the TA hasn't cared much about that. Their new leader has brought a lot of change, and most of it bad."

"Who is that?" Heather asked.

"Sophie Blackhart. She got elected into the post about a year ago, but it feels like it's been longer than that, looking at how many things she's changed."

"Is she Fabio's daughter?"

"His niece. Fabio died a couple of years ago, then we had Qohrie Chavez in between, but he died prematurely."

Heather lifted an eyebrow. "Suspicious circumstances?"

"Some people think so," the Archivist replied in a low voice.

"Could we stop talking about politics and focus on Hjalmar instead?" I interjected. "Do I understand this correctly, they hacked his bracelet, pulled him back into the present and imprisoned him? For murder?"

He nodded. "I doubt they knew about you being there with him until you didn't return to class. There's been quite a search going on for you, so you better stay out of sight unless you want to be interrogated. Or expelled. I don't spend enough time in the teachers' common room to know what they have planned for you."

"Where do they think I am?" I asked. "If they knew I was in the Viking past, why didn't they send anyone to come and get me?"

"Hjalmar's bracelet fried when they got him here; so

they don't know where exactly he's been. And there are some teachers who think we shouldn't invest resources into finding a student who broke all the rules."

From the way he looked at me, he made it very clear that he was one of those people. In a way, he was probably right. I had broken the rules, but when I'd decided to go with Hjalmar, those rules had seemed insignificant compared to the prospect of meeting Vikings.

"We need to find out where he's being held," Heather said. "And what exactly he's accused of. Since I'm his mother, I'm best set to ask those questions. Lainie, you need to stay hidden for now. Asger, same goes for you. You're not used to the people of this time and their scheming. You've been raised to be honourable, just like Hjalmar, but people nowadays don't always respect the code you follow. Archivist, would you mind bringing me to the headmistress? I think I need to have a word with her."

He bowed his head. I was amazed by how nice he was to Heather. I didn't think he had it in him. Then he turned to me, his eyes blazing with annoyance, and I deleted that thought. He was an arse.

"Stay here," he snapped. "Don't touch anything. If I see so much as a fingerprint on my desk, I'm going to send you back into the past and will make sure you stay there."

I was speechless. Did he really think that badly of me? I was going to have to change his opinion of me. I wanted him to like me, for some strange reason. Maybe it was because I loved a challenge, and the Archivist was the ultimate challenge.

Heather got up and smoothed down her dress. Her long hair was braided around her head, making it look a bit like a diadem. She was stunning. I didn't have any doubt that she'd be able to find out all the information she wanted. She knew how to handle herself; after all, she'd lived in Norse society for decades, where women didn't have as many rights as they did in the present.

She said a few words to Asger in Old Norse. The only words I picked out were Hjalmar's and my names.

"Don't touch anything," the Archivist repeated and stormed out of the room without gracing me with another look. How rude.

"I'll see if I can get us some food on the way back," Heather promised, making me aware of how empty my stomach was. Probably because I'd emptied its contents on the Archivist's shoes. Which he hadn't cleaned properly yet. Poor guy. Maybe that was the cause of his bad mood.

"Alone," Asger grunted in his heavily accented voice. "What doing?"

Good question. Who knew how long the other two would be gone?

I guessed we could sneak into the Archive and do some exploring, although I doubted the Archivist would be happy about that. He'd probably hate me even more if I did that. The alternative was staying put and wait. Boring.

The time travel had made me tired, but I was way too wired to sleep. So many questions, so many problems to solve. Somewhere, Hjalmar was sitting in a cell for a crime he hadn't committed.

I allowed myself a small smile. At least he wasn't dead or lost in time. Maybe we could break him out of prison. Or get him out the legal way. Probably better, especially if the Archivist was helping us. He seemed to be a stickler for rules.

Asger put a large arm around my shoulders. Blacksmithing had done more to his physique than a gym ever could. I remembered how I had explored his body in my dream. In *our* dream. It had felt so real. Even now, it seemed like a recent memory, not the fading fragments dreams usually left behind. I could almost taste him on my lips.

I let him pull me against his chest and snuggled into his embrace. Maybe this time should be used for bonding. Verifying if my dream had been accurate. A scientific experiment.

"Fuck?" he asked, just like he'd done this morning.

I laughed.

"Maybe."

CHAPTER 17

It felt weird doing this in the Archive, in a dusty room that neither of us had ever been in. The Archivist and Heather could come back any minute. And yet, I craved to touch Asger. His chest was hard against my cheek, his heartbeat a constant drumming in my ear. His shirt was rough fabric, nowhere near as soft as a modern shirt would have been, but it suited him. Rough on the outside, but soft on the inside. He'd already proven that.

I hardly knew him, yet that dream had formed a strange bond between us. It'd shown me a future that could happen if I let him close. In the dream, I'd already made the choice. Already committed to him. Now, I had to decide if I wanted it to happen in the present as well.

I lifted my head and looked at him. He blinked down at me and his lips curved into a gentle smile.

"Lainie," he whispered, pronouncing my name in an exotic, beautiful way. I wanted to ask him to repeat it again and again, but it seemed a little silly.

"Asger," I replied, my voice husky. Before I could further debate whether this was a good idea, he bent down and pressed his lips to mine. He tasted exactly like he had in the dream. In the memory. Whatever it had been.

I opened my mouth, letting him in. His kiss was hard and fast, without any hesitation at all. He wanted this as much as I did. All thoughts fled my mind as I returned his kiss with the same passion. It felt like I'd kissed him a hundred times before. Familiar. Like home. For some reason, I knew exactly where he liked to be touched, how he wanted me to respond, what sounds he made when I nibbled on his bottom lip. Past, present and future were getting muddled up, but I didn't care, as long as I was in Asger's arms.

Never moving his lips from mine, he put his hands on my hips and lifted me up in one strong motion, settling me on his lap. Despite the hardness of his muscles, he was surprisingly comfy. I melted into his embrace, his kiss all I could think about. When had life become so wonderful?

His tongue danced with mine, his lips fought against my own. We were united in this battle of kisses, pausing only for occasional ragged breaths. The way he held me was driving me crazy. His warmth went straight through my skin and into my heart.

I slipped my hands underneath his shirt, not caring that one of the buttons bounced off and fell to the floor. I'm sure Asger would be able to fix it. And if not... better view for me. His belly was flat as a board, despite this bulk, so I wouldn't mind looking at it more often. His skin was hot beneath his clothes. Maybe I should help him out of those, make him a little cooler. And give me the benefit of the view.

"Take off your shirt," I whispered.

"You too," he replied with a wink. Cheeky Viking. I got up, cursing my jumpsuit. There was no way to elegantly pull it over my head. I had to step out of the whole thing, leaving me bare. Maybe that wasn't such a bad thing; the others might return soon so we had to be quick about it.

I took off my shoes and shimmied out of my jumpsuit. My bra was a pretty lace one, but my panties were unsightly knickers that Heather had given me. I guess Hjalmar wasn't used to modern lingerie though, or he simply didn't care, because he stared at me with so much desire in his eyes that I launched myself at him, ending up in his arms once again. He'd taken off his shirt and skin met skin, just before our lips joined into another passionate kiss. He pulled me into his lap until I was straddling him, my breasts pressed against his chest. His erection pushed against my core, stopped from entering me only by the fact that he was still wearing trousers. I wanted him so badly.

His hands ran up and down my back, then settled on my bum. I squealed when he squeezed my cheeks, and he groaned as I jerked my hips against his cock.

"I want you," I whispered, our lips still touching.

"Fuck?" he asked with a cheeky wink.

"Fuck," I confirmed. Then stopped smiling.

Fuck. "I don't suppose you have a condom?" I asked, hating to break the moment.

"Condom?"

Urgh, of course he had no idea what that was, and I wasn't about to launch into a lecture on contraception. I doubted he'd have a problem with me becoming pregnant, but I did. I had only just started my studies and I was determined to finish them, preferably without a baby to look after.

"It's to stop you from making me pregnant," I explained. And to stop me from getting any Viking diseases, but I didn't say that. I had to ask Heather about that. Not that I assumed Asger to have an STI, but better safe than sorry.

He nodded in understanding. "I can... feel good."

Before I could clarify what he was trying to say, he flipped me onto my back and ripped off my panties. Yes, actually ripped them to pieces. Now I really was bare for him. He smiled down at me, then spread my legs, his eyes greedily focusing on my core.

Was he going to...

Yes, he was. He slipped off the sofa and kneeled in front of me.

"Feel good," he repeated, spreading my legs a little wider. Cool air hit my core, making me shiver, but then his lips were there, kissing me in that most intimate place. Heat shot through me and I arched my back, barely able to stop myself from moaning.

He traced a line of soft kisses along my sensitive skin, before following the same path with his tongue. That alone almost made me come. He flicked my bud with his tongue before starting to kiss me again. His beard tickled my skin, but it was surprisingly soft. I'd thought it would be all scratchy, but in fact, it only added to the sensation.

Flick. Kiss. Flick. Kiss.

He was driving me crazy, not quite giving me enough to come but keeping me teetering on the edge, breathless and moaning.

He grabbed my thighs tighter, then buried himself into me, his entire face pressed against my entrance, his tongue inside of me. When he moved his tongue, swirling it around my core, I could no longer hold back. I came with a scream, rocking against him, willing him to keep touching me.

Just when I thought it couldn't get any better, he pushed a finger inside of me while at the same time sucking sharply on my bud. I unravelled, letting go of any self-control I still had.

This was heaven.

I STRAIGHTENED MY CLOTHES, trying to make it look as if I didn't just have a hot encounter with Asger. There was nothing I could do about my flushed skin though. I ran my fingers through my tangled hair. Asger seemed to have a thing about ruffling my hair, which meant that I could really do with a brush. In the end though, none of that mattered.

Hjalmar was imprisoned somewhere and here I was, making out with his brother. I wondered what Hjalmar would have to say about this frille thing. Somehow, I couldn't imagine someone like him consent to sharing, but at the same time, he'd grown up in another time. He might like the thought of sharing me with his brother. An image flashed into my mind, me being held by both of them, our naked bodies pressed together. A shiver of excitement ran down my back and heat pooled between my legs. Even though Asger had just made me come in the most amazing way, the thought of being with both brothers at once made me almost ready to come again.

Maybe it was selfish, greedy, perhaps it was what I should do. There was no way to know until I actually did it. For now, I was going to keep an open mind.

ᚠᚼᛒᛁᛏᚢᚠᛁ 18

T he sound of the secret passage door opening made me sit up straight and once again smooth down my uniform. Heather was Asger's mother, after all. It was kind of strange to be in the same room with her after I'd had Asger between my legs.

The Archivist stormed into our little room, his eyes flicking to my flushed cheeks and his expression turned even darker. Well, excuse me. He'd told me not to touch anything, but there had been no rule about me being touched. Besides, it wasn't like he should care about what I did in my spare time, even if it was getting up close with Vikings.

Heather gave me a knowing smile. Thank goodness, she wasn't reacting in the way my own mother would have. With embarrassment and barely concealed bewilderment. I think my father had been the only man my mother had ever been with, and I couldn't imagine them doing anything more than vanilla.

Not that I had any more experience. Despite that

dream, despite Hjalmar, despite having Asger pleasure me, I was still a virgin. I didn't feel like it.

I pushed away those thoughts and focused on what was important. Hjalmar.

"Did you find him?" I asked Heather, ignoring the Archivist. I didn't feel like being glared at.

She nodded, but she didn't look happy. "We've come just in time. He's still here at the Academy, but they're planning to transfer him to the TA prison tomorrow. Headmistress Tape has fought to persuade the TA to let him stay here until the trial, but they're refusing to listen to her."

"Which is a bad sign," the Archivist mutters. "The TTA headmasters have always had a position of authority, of respect. For the Head of the Time Agency to simply ignore Professor Tape's request shows just how bad things have become."

"I'm going to speak to Sophie Blackhart," Heather declared. "I met her a couple of times when I was still working as an agent. She might listen to reason."

The Archivist laughs. "I don't think so. If she doesn't listen to the head of the TTA, the most prestigious academy in the world, then I doubt she'll listen to a retired time agent who's not been seen in decades. Sorry, love, but I don't think you have a chance in hell to change that woman's mind."

Heather frowns but doesn't argue. She probably knows that he's right.

"What do we do then?" I ask. "Can we break him out while he's still here?"

"Kill all," Asger suggests.

"I don't think that will work," Heather says with a sad

smile. "It's not how we do things here, Asger. We need to go through the official channels."

"Can't we just travel back in time to the day they brought him here and arrested him? We might have a chance to free him before they put him in a cell."

The Archivist shakes his head. "The agents who arrested him will have TDs. There's no way to approach without being noticed."

"TDs?" I ask.

He sighs in exasperation. "Don't you know anything? Time Detectors. They recognise ripples in time, which means they know someone is about to time travel to their location a few seconds before it happens. It would give them enough time to either ready their weapons or hurry Hjalmar into a cell. Either or, it wouldn't work."

"But what if we arrive in a different part of the Academy? Are those TDs sensitive enough to pick up the ripples even if we're several floors above them?"

"Yes, they can detect ripples in a radius of about a mile, so there's no chance to arrive in the Academy without being detected. The only reason you managed to land here unscathed earlier was because you had the bracelet of a TTA student. Without it, you would have ended up somewhere above ground in the official reception centre. Which is swarming with security."

"What if I travel back in time on my own and arrive just after Hjalmar and I left?" I ask. "That way, I would never have left, could go to my lessons, pretend to know nothing and figure out a way to get to Hjalmar."

This time, the Archivist rolls his eyes. "There's been a search going on for you. Your plan may have worked if only one or two people noticed your absence, but your disappearance has affected too many people. It would change time too much."

I scoff. "Then what do we do? We can't just sit here and wait. Twiddling our thumbs isn't going to get Hjalmar back."

"The only thing we can do is prove his innocence," Heather says softly. "But if we do that, we might endanger someone's life." She raises an eyebrow at the Archivist.

I realise that he wouldn't know about Lucas still being alive. Nobody does except for the three of us and Hjalmar.

"So, he's definitely innocent?" the Archivist asks.

Heather nods. "He never killed anyone."

"But he won't be able to prove it in court?"

She nods again. "He'll never tell them the truth. He'd sentence someone to death by doing so, and he's far too honourable for that. He'd rather go to prison for life."

I shudder at the thought. I'd never see him again. They don't have a reason to admit a student to see her imprisoned teacher. I'm not related to him, not in an official relationship either. There needs to be something we can do. I can't let this happen to him.

"What if we remove the reason he can't tell the truth?" I ask and they all stare at me in confusion.

"Right now, he can't because he'd endanger someone's life. What if we made sure that this someone wouldn't be danger should he be found alive? That way, Hjalmar's name would be cleared."

It's a stab in the dark, really. I still don't know why Lucas might be killed if he returned to the present. It must be something terrible, after all, Lucas sacrificed an arm for it.

"I doubt that would work," Heather said. "From what I know, there are too many people who want him dead. Too many to deal with. Besides, what would we do with them? We can't kill them."

Yeah, that was true. Morals. For a moment, I'd forgotten that we couldn't just go around and kill people who prevented me from being with Hjalmar. When had I turned so infatuated with him? So possessive?

"If we're talking about Lucas Demarque, then it might not be as hard as you think," the Archivist said, and I perked up. "Things have changed since the boy disappeared."

"What do you mean?" Heather asked.

"I don't know the full story, but I always thought it was very convenient for Lucas to die when he did. And that there was no reason for Hjalmar to kill him. Lucas was a bright lad; he spent a lot of time helping me out in the Archive. He behaved very strangely the last time I saw him. Said something about regretting what he'd done. I didn't think much of it back then, I thought it was something menial, something to do with his studies or maybe that he'd fallen out with his boyfriend. Of course, my view on that changed when he disappeared."

He sighed deeply. "I did some investigating after that. He'd been one of my best helpers and I didn't believe that he had just got lost in time. He was talented, destined to rise quickly through the TA ranks. For him to make a mistake during time travel seemed like a strange excuse. And I wasn't the only one to think that. The days after his disappearance, the Academy was crawling with agents. Usually, the Academy itself deals with accidents to students. This was different."

"That's why Hjalmar had to prove that Lucas was

dead," Heather explained. "He'd planned to take some blood-drenched clothes back to the present, but then Lucas had the accident and we had a spare arm."

Asger chuckled. "Idiot."

"Wait, so Hjalmar didn't cut off Lucas's arm?" I interjected.

Heather laughed. "Did he tell you that? No, it was an accident. Lucas tried to impress one of the Vikings in the village by challenging him to a fight. He boasted that he was an excellent fighter, so they used sharp weapons. Sadly for Lucas, he was quite good at attacking but rubbish at keeping his guard up. Modern doctors could have probably saved his arm, but since he refused to be returned to the present, our village healer had to amputate."

"Idiot," Asger repeated. He seemed to be able to follow our conversation even though it was all in English. Seemed like he'd pretended not to understand me back at his house. I was going to find a way to seek revenge for that, just you wait.

"It was a good move," the Archivist said. "Things quieted down when Hjalmar returned with the arm. Of course, most people thought that he'd killed the boy because they'd had a public argument a couple of weeks prior, but Professor Tape believed him, trusted him. She even tried to stop the rumour that Hjalmar was a murderer from spreading, but this is TTA after all. This place thrives on gossip."

"You said you did some investigating." I tried to get the conversation back to the important bit. Finding a way to save Hjalmar. "Did you find out who wanted Lucas dead?"

"His stepmother," Heather whispered before the Archivist could reply.

I gaped at her. "Is this a fairy tale? The evil stepmother?"

"That's what I thought," the Archivist confirmed. "Lucas used a fake surname when he was enrolled here, but after a bit of digging I found his real name. No wonder he was scared. His father had just died, and he was the last block in his stepmother's aim to get her hands on her husband's business empire."

"Definitely a fairy tale," I muttered. "So, he's being hunted because he inherited a bit of money?"

Heather laughed bitterly. "A bit of money doesn't quite cut it. His father was Richard Priest."

"Priest? Like Priest Enterprises?"

"Exactly, that Richard Priest," the Archivist said. "Multi-billionaire, serial tax avoider and, if you believe the rumours, involved in far too many shady businesses."

"No wonder Lucas used a pseudonym. I once went on a protest march to raise awareness on the monopoly Priest Enterprises had on the electricity supply in New London. Nobody likes the Priests." I ran a hand through my tousled hair. "So, this woman, his stepmother, is the only person wanting him dead?"

The Archivist school his head. "Not quite. Back when his father died, Pricilla Priest put a bounty on the lad's head, which meant that hundreds of people would have been looking for him. Criminals, corrupt agents, you name it. Money can be a fantastic motivator, especially if the bounty is ten million."

I couldn't help but gasp. "Ten million? To kill Lucas?"

He nodded. "And to make it look like an accident, obviously. In a way, Hjalmar did that woman a favour.

Lucas was declared dead and Pricilla got all the money. She didn't even come to his funeral."

"Lucas had a funeral?"

"We had it here at the Academy. It was a beautiful ceremony." The Archivist's expression turned distant. "A lot of people said nice things about him. It was hard to believe that anyone would want him dead."

I wondered if Lucas knew about his funeral. It was kind of strange, being alive yet knowing that everyone thought you were dead. Although it had saved his life, and even though he was trapped back in time, he was still alive. And had Vikings to seduce. I smiled at the thought. I hoped he would get the Viking of his dreams. As long as he didn't take one of mine.

I leaned back, my mind spinning. It seemed so complicated. To free Hjalmar, we'd have to expose Lucas, which would mean his stepmother would once again put a bounty on his head. Hiding him in the past wouldn't be a solution this time; I doubted this trick would work a second time. Lucas would soon run out of limbs. Still, I couldn't let Hjalmar rot in prison.

"You were right," I said to the Archivist as an idea slowly began to form in my mind.

He raised an eyebrow. "I was?"

"Money is a great motivator. We need to talk to Priscilla Priest. If she wants to keep Lucas's inheritance, she'll be interested in keeping it quiet that he's still alive. If she used her money to somehow create an alibi for Hjalmar, or to bribe people to get him out of jail, he'd never be tempted to tell the court that Lucas is still alive."

Heather's expression brightened a little. "That could work. I bet she's closely following the trial already. If we managed to get to her, make her worried that her rich days are over, she might act in our favour."

"Or kill us all," the Archivist muttered darkly. "As long as there are people alive who know the truth, she'll be in danger to lose her empire."

"What if we get Lucas to write an official letter stating that he gives up any claim to his inheritance?" I suggested. "And we could also leave some statements of our own with lawyers, to be published if one of us gets killed." I shuddered at the thought. This moment seemed very important. Dramatic. I kind of wanted to giggle to diffuse the tension building within me.

"That could work," Heather said. "It's risky, but we don't have another plan. I can travel back and talk to Lucas, while you go and talk to Priscilla Priest. Asger, do you want to return home with me? I don't think you'll be able to help with the negotiations."

"I stay," Asger grunted. "I defend."

He put an arm on my thigh, making it very clear who he was planning to protect. I smiled at him. Even though Heather was right, it was good to know that Asger was going to be by my side.

"How are we going to meet her?" I asked. "Can we just turn up at her place?"

The Archivist laughed. "We'd end up as dog food before we even set foot in her house. No, let me get in touch with some contacts. They'll be able to set up a meeting."

I stared at him in surprise. "Contacts? Like, criminal contacts?"

He shrugged. "You didn't think I built the Archive's collection all by legal means, did you?"

I closed my eyes, surrendering to the stream of hot water kneading my tired muscles. The Archivist had the most amazing shower, miles better than the ones we had in our communal student bathrooms. I was only slightly jealous.

Rather than stay with the teachers on the top floor of the Academy, he had his own little studio flat just next door from the Archive. Since I didn't want to be seen, this was perfect for cleaning up and feel human again. I didn't know how Heather had survived for decades without hot showers. Or maybe she'd built her own, who knew. I'd been too tired last night to ask for anything more than the cloth and the bowl of warm water she'd given me.

I stretched my arms and arched my back against the wall. The hot water helped soothe the tension in my body, but it didn't quite remove it completely. A voice in the back of my mind kept telling me that I needed to hurry, that Hjalmar was imprisoned, that I shouldn't be enjoying a long hot shower. At the same time, I knew there was nothing I could do but wait for the Archivist to set up the meeting with Priscilla Priest. Heather had returned to the past, using a time bracelet the Archivist had given her, which would allow her to travel right back into the Archive - something normal bracelets couldn't do since this floor of the building was shielded somehow. I'd asked how that worked but all the Archivist had done was glare at me as if it was my fault that nobody has taught us stuff like that.

I switched off the shower and wrapped myself into a towel that the Archivist had given me. I grimaced. Here I was, in his shower, smelling like him thanks to his masculine shower gel, and I didn't even know his name. Did every Archivist give up their own name, or was this a special quirk of the current one? Maybe his name was so awful, so embarrassing, that he preferred others not to know it.

Twisting my hair into a messy, wet bun, I wondered whether it was safe to leave the bathroom. The Archivist had said he'd get me some clothes in my size, but I wasn't sure if he'd done that yet. I opened the door an inch wide and peeked outside. Nobody to be seen. Maybe he'd already put the new jumpsuit somewhere for me to find. Barefoot and still a little wet, I traipsed across his living room.

The kitchenette in the corner looked mostly unused, even though I'd never seen the Archivist in the dining hall. Maybe he had his food delivered down here rather than eat with everyone else. It would certainly fit his antisocial personality.

A bed with messy sheets and a plethora of pillows was on the other side of the room. Someone should teach this guy how to make a bed. My mother would be appalled at how untidy it looked.

"What the fuck are you doing?"

I swirled around, stumbled, fell. My towel unravelled and ended up around my waist, leaving my chest bare. I looked up at the Archivist, who'd entered the studio without me realising. I jumped to my feet, my boobs bouncing, only making it worse. The towel fell to the floor. I was naked, bare in front of the one man who I really didn't want to see me this vulnerable. For some reason, I wanted him to think that I was strong, but being naked wasn't conducive to that in the slightest.

I clutched my arms in front of my chest, then realised what else was naked and put a hand between my legs.

My skin had to be bright red by now, and all I wanted was to sink into the ground and never face him again. I dared a quick glance at his expression - and couldn't help but look again and again. His eyes were fixed on me, his pupils strangely dilated. His expression was tense, as if he was trying to control himself. He couldn't hide the desire in his gaze though, the way he seemed to devour my body with his eyes.

My skin seemed to burn wherever his attention fell. My nipples pressed hard against my arm, reminding me that I was trying to hide my assets, not let him stare at them. I made a squeaky sound, a mixture of panic and embarrassment. That was it, the moment was gone.

The Archivist pointed to my feet. "Towel," he said drily, without turning around to give me some privacy. Was the bastard enjoying this?

My eyes fell to his crotch. His black jeans were tight, but there was an obvious bulge between his legs. This was arousing him. It kind of made me feel better. In a way, I had power over him. I was the one who could decide to hide behind a towel or to stay naked. Not the best choice ever, but it gave me a bit of confidence.

"Turn around," I told him, more an order than a suggestion.

"No."

He crossed his arms in front of his chest. He'd changed into a black shirt with rolled up sleeves, leaving his arms exposed. He had a tattooed snake circling across his left upper arm, wrapped around him in a strangling embrace. It looked beautiful from afar and I was tempted to ask him if I could have a closer look. I'd always wanted a tattoo myself, but with money being tight, that had been very low on my list of priorities. Maybe once I graduated from TTA. *If* that was ever going to happen. The way things were looking just now, chances were I'd never even get to finish my first term.

"Fine." Rather than give him the view of my boobs, I turned before bending down to pick up the towel. I hoped he got the message. Kiss my arse.

"You're asking to be spanked," he muttered under his breath. His voice had changed to a husky tenor, making me all warm and squishy inside. That man was going to be the end of me. As if two Vikings weren't enough trouble. Now here I was, lusting after a man whose name I didn't know, who I knew nothing about at all.

Now that I finally had my towel back, I wrapped it around me as tightly as I could. He'd seen enough, I didn't want to give him another opportunity.

"Did you bring me some clothes?" I demanded more forcefully than I'd intended.

He pointed to the bathroom door. There, right next to the door, they lay in a neat pile. I was such an idiot.

His lips curved into a taunting smile. "Do you need help getting dressed?"

In response, I snatched up the clothes and disappeared into the bathroom, banging the door shut as hard as I could. Inside, I leaned against the tiled wall, the coldness of it giving my flushed skin some relief. My nipples were still hard and thinking about the Archivist on the other side of this door didn't help with that. Was he going to touch himself to get rid of that erection? I kind of hoped he would. He'd be thinking of me, even if he was annoyed about me.

I shook my head, disappointed of my own thoughts. I was trying to rescue Hjalmar to be with him. I also wanted to be with Asger. And now, after seeing the way the Archivist had looked at me... I was a lost cause. Maybe I should become a nun. Have no man instead of three. That might save my heart from being torn into three pieces. Or maybe two, in case I was misinterpreting the Archivist's behaviour.

Slamming my hand against the wall, I pushed those thoughts away, far away, then hid them behind a wall, then built another, higher wall, then threw a whole load of stones on top of them. I was going to be sensible, strong, successful. And I was going to rescue Hjalmar without getting distracted.

I put on my clothes as quickly as possible, then pressed my ear against the door. No sounds that suggested the Archivist was still in the living room. That gave me hope. I didn't want to be alone with him again, not for quite some time. I'd just be a blushing, stammering idiot, especially if his grey eyes were full of barely held back desire as they had been before. A shiver ran over my skin at the thought. A very, very pleasant shiver.

With Heather gone, it was just Asger and the Archivist in the dusty little room. Asger was still wearing the same clothes as before, but then, his weren't ripped and covered in puke. I shot a quick glance at the Archivist's shoes. They were different ones than before. Not the ones I decorated with the contents of my stomach. I almost thought about offering to clean that other pair, but no, not right now. He'd probably come up with some form of torture to add to the humiliation.

"My contact has arranged a meeting point for us," the Archivist said once I'd taken a seat. "Before we go there, we'll each write down what we know about Lucas and Hjalmar, and then I'll hand those to Professor Tape for safekeeping."

"Trust she? Good woman?" Asger asked. His sentences were getting longer; he seemed to be picking up the confidence to try out more of his English vocabulary.

"Yes, I trust her with my life," the Archivist said, his voice solemn. "She saved my life once, and I doubt she would endanger it now." He handed us both a piece of paper and a pen. Asger looked at both in confusion, but then, after watching me starting to write, he took the pen and put it to paper. And ripped it into shreds. He'd clearly never used a pen before and was using far too much force.

I took his hand and showed him how to hold the pen, how to gently glide it over the paper. His skin was rough, showing years of hard labour as a smith, but despite the size of his hands, he gripped the pen with a strange gentleness.

This time, he managed to scribble some runes. The Younger Futhark, I noticed. Hjalmar would be proud of me. Although, maybe not. I'd been terrible at understanding anything the Vikings had said in Old Norse back in the past, even though I'd memorised over two hundred words already. I needed to work on my pronunciation, clearly it had been entirely different from how the words were actually said.

I left Asger to it and wrote my own statement. Most of what I knew was second hand, but I had seen Lucas alive, I had seen that he was missing an arm. I wrote down as much as I could think of, then signed it with a flourish before handing it to the Archivist.

Once Asger had finished - his paper looked a mess but maybe someone would be able to make sense of it - the Archivist put all three in an envelope and sealed it.

"We're going to port to the Headmistress's office," the Archivist announced. "I don't want either of you to be seen, it would raise too many questions and we don't have time to explain. It's a miracle that I was able to arrange an immediate meeting with Priscilla Priest in the first place, so we really don't want to keep her waiting."

He'd put on a large time bracer which covered most of his snake tattoo.

"Can you port two people at a time?" I asked curiously. "I thought it was only one at a time."

"It's possible for short distances," he explained while entering coordinates via the holographic keyboard now hovering above his arm. "But we're going to need to borrow an additional bracelet for travelling to our meeting. Berlin isn't exactly next door."

"Berlin?" Asger asked in confusion.

"Germany," I explained, but that didn't seem to mean anything to him either. "A large city in another country."

"City," he said with a grin, proud that he understood that word. I smiled at him, wanting to ruffle his hair and cuddle him like a massive, adorable teddy bear. Then I reminded myself that he was a fearsome Viking with hands large enough to squash my skull, and decided not to.

The Archivist stretched out his arm. "Hold on tight, although this will feel like a walk in the park compared to the journey you did earlier today."

Gingerly, I put my hand on his arm. Not because I was concerned about the porting, but because I was worried about what touching him might do to me. He met my eyes and winked. That bastard. He probably knew how uncomfortable this was making me.

Asger put his hand on mine and then we were off, drenched in sunlight, bathed in warmth, before tumbling back into reality. That had been my shortest travel so far. When I'd first come to the Academy, the porting from New London to here had taken a few minutes, although it was hard to tell since time seemed to lose all meaning while flying through space. Reaching the Headmistress's office had taken mere seconds.

We were in a small waiting room adjacent to Professor Tape's actual office.

"Let me handle this," the Archivist said, and before I could react or argue, he walked into the office and closed the door behind him.

Asger looked at me and shrugged. "Strange man."

I laughed. "Yes, you could say that. He's a very strange man."

Just when I'd decided to sit down on one of the uncomfortable looking chairs, the Archivist returned, closing the door before I could get a glimpse of the Headmistress.

"All done, she's put our statements in the safe," he reported, already typing in new coordinates into his bracer. When he's done, he hands Asger a smaller bracelet and the Viking expertly snaps it around his wrist.

"What about me?" I ask.

The Archivist smirks at me. "You travel with me."

He's at my side in an instant, wrapping an arm around my waist and pulling me close. His scent is familiar; thanks to his shower gel I smell the same. I don't know what to do. Push him away, tell him that I don't want to be hugged like that? Or lean into his body, enjoy the moment?

Luckily, I don't have to decide. He presses a button and bright light embraces us.

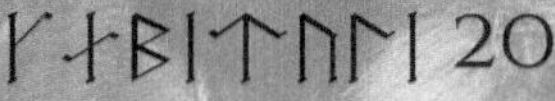

When the Archivist mentioned Berlin, I was thinking of the Brandenburg Gate, the rebuilt City Palace, the Reichstag. Instead, we were in a park, surrounded by trees, flower beds and a couple of fountains that had seen better days. This didn't feel like a city at all. There were no people anywhere close, just a few lone souls milling far in the distance.

The Archivist tapped around on his bracer. "It's the right location," he confirmed. "Maybe we're early."

Suddenly, someone appeared out of thin air right in front of us. Asger was in front of me before I could even blink, ready to defend me. Oh, my sweet Viking.

"No, you're late."

A broad man in a tailored black suit was examining us, probably evaluating how much of a threat we were. His eyes lingered on Asger for a moment, then he lifted his wrist to his mouth.

"All clear, they're unarmed."

Did he have some kind of x-ray vision to know that?

With a flash of light, three more people ported to our little group. Two men with exactly the same suits, flanking a woman. That had to be Pricilla Priest. She was a short woman, maybe an inch or two above five foot. Her grey hair was styled in an elegant bun, topped with a pearl comb. There were more pearls around her neck and her wrists. It looked like she'd even turned her porting bracelet into an homage to pearls. Her face was caked in a thick layer of makeup, not the flattering kind. It actually made her seem older. Her body was wrapped in a pink coat that hid most of her figure. She looked ready for winter, even though it was barely late spring.

She turned to the Archivist. "You're the one who wanted to meet?"

He nodded.

"What's so important that I had to leave my house? Be quick, I have Sheikh Ali come over for tea in half an hour."

The Archivist's eyes flicked to the three men surrounding Pricilla. "I don't think you'll want anyone to hear what I have to say."

"Ma'am," one of her guards warned, but she waved him off.

"Alright, but be aware, I don't suffer fools lightly. If this isn't worth my time, I might shorten your own time considerably."

The Archivist bowed his head, although I could see the tension in him rise. "Understood."

"If my men leave, your big guy here has to go with them. The girl can stay."

Asger opened his mouth to protest, but I squeezed his hand. "We'll be fine," I whispered. "Don't worry."

He muttered something in Old Norse, but then walked away, following the three men in suits.

I really hoped that we were doing the right thing here. It was risky and could end in tears and death. Still, it was the only option we had. I couldn't let Hjalmar stay in prison, punished for something he didn't do. At the same time, I didn't want to have Lucas's death on my conscience either. Negotiating with this woman was a necessary evil.

Once the men were out of earshot, the Archivist cleared his throat. "We have some information on your stepson."

Wow. I would have started with some small talk, check out her mood and then decide how best to broach the subject. Instead, he'd just jumped right into it.

She laughed, but her eyes were cold and calculating. "Lucas? He's dead. There was a funeral, such a lovely ceremony, or so I've heard. Sadly, I couldn't make it there myself, such a busy schedule, you know?"

I wanted to wipe that smile off her face. How dare she laugh about Lucas's supposed death.

Taking a page out of the Archivist's book, I hit her with the truth. "He's still alive."

Her eyes widened slightly. "No, you're mistaken. He was killed on a time travel mission. His teacher was only able to bring back part of his body, the rest was taken by savages."

"That teacher is currently in prison, waiting to be trialled for murder," the Archivist explained, taking over from me. "But what if he were to tell the judges the truth? That Lucas is still alive?"

"He can't be alive," Priscilla spluttered. "He would have returned by now to claim his inheritance."

I couldn't help but tsk. "You don't seem to know your stepson at all. He's not interested in the money, all he wants is to live his life, preferably alive."

Her gaze turned poisonous. "You have no proof. I'm not going to believe two random people who I don't know anything about. You might just be here to black-mail me. Trust me, you wouldn't be the first."

I smiled and pulled a piece of paper from my pocket; the shopping list Lucas had written. "Do you recognise your stepson's handwriting?"

She snatched the paper from my hand and stared at it. A slight tremor shook her hand as she studied it. When she finally handed it back to me, her expression was guarded.

"You want him killed? The teacher?"

"No, we want him released from prison," I said quickly before she got the wrong idea.

She chuckled. "And what would give you the idea that I could do that?"

"You're one of the richest women in the world. I'm sure you have your ways," I shot back.

"The richest, actually," she corrected. "But tell me, what would make me want to invest into getting him out of prison? It would be much easier to simply have him removed from the equation."

I tried very hard not to glare at her and kick her in the private parts.

"Because if he dies, if any of us die, proof that he is alive will be sent not only to the authorities, but also to the press," the Archivist said. "There will be inquests, investigations, lots of problems for you. I doubt you'll be able to silence them all, even with all your money."

"You're playing a risky game," Priscilla hissed, no

longer pretending to be polite. "And what is giving me the guarantee that Lucas won't simply turn up in a year's time, alive and well?"

"We will be able to provide you with a written statement from Lucas, signed by witnesses, stating that he relinquishes all claims to his inheritance, and that he will stay dead."

"Until your death," I quickly added, hoping that this might give Lucas the chance of returning to the present, if he ever chose to do so.

The woman met my eyes and we stared at each other. I was having a hard time not to blink, but I wasn't going to be the one to back down.

"Until my natural death," she corrected, not taking her eyes off me.

"Deal."

She sighed. "I assume you want that man out of jail immediately?"

I flashed her a smile. "You assume correctly."

When we returned to the Archive, Heather was there waiting for us, clutching the statement Lucas had written.

"He's so relieved that this might soon be over, even if he won't be able to return back home. I think he's still secretly been scared that someone might find and kill him."

The Archivist took the statement and read through it, a smile beginning to curve on his lips. "That's exactly what we needed. I shall send Priscilla Priest a virtual copy of it for now and then bring the original with us when she tells us where to meet her and Hjalmar."

Heather's eyes flashed with happiness, her expression brightening as if the sun had suddenly appeared down here in the basement. "You made it? She's getting him out of there?"

I nodded. "She said it might take a few hours, but he'll be back with us by the end of the day. For now, all we can do is wait." I cleared my throat, a little uncomfortable about the thoughts running through my mind. "Do you think he'll be able to stay here? Or is it better if he lays low in Viking times for a while?"

Heather gave me a sympathetic smile. "Let's not sharpen our axes prematurely. I doubt he's going to let us make a decision for him. Hjalmar has always done what he wants, and this isn't going to change now."

The Archivist had been listening to our conversation from afar, but now he stepped closer, his expression unreadable.

"Lainie. A word."

I looked at him in surprise, but then followed him into his studio flat. I was way too intrigued to do anything else.

As soon as I'd closed the door behind me, he turned and stepped towards me, invading my personal space.

"Hjalmar will be back soon," he whispered, his eyes roaming up and down my body. "Then you'll have two Vikings vying for your attention."

I laughed, trying to diffuse the tension that was building between us. He was too close, this was too intense. I was fighting both the urge to touch him and to run away. This man was doing things to me that I couldn't control.

"Are you going to give me dating advice?" I joked, my voice trembling. "Tell me who to choose?"

His ashen eyes turned to molten silver. "No. I'm going to stake my claim before it's too late."

And then he kissed me.

CHAPTER 21

The Archivist's kiss was hot and scalding. Nothing remained of the cold demeanour he'd shown all day. Maybe I should have stopped him, protested that he couldn't treat me like a thief and then change his mind and kiss me, but I wasn't able to fight the urge to kiss him back, to give myself to him. I needed him, wanted him.

His kiss was more than just a simple lips-on-lips. He claimed me, made sure I knew that he wasn't going to let the two Vikings have me to themselves. Just like he'd said, he was staking his claim. And I was happy to let him. While I knew Asger and Hjalmar so much better than the Archivist, I'd felt a strange attraction to him ever since I bumped into him in the corridor. He was strange and unusual and exotic. The mystery surrounding him only increased the pull I felt towards him.

He pressed me against the wall, his body hard against mine. For someone who spent every day in an underground archive, he was surprisingly fit. Not that I was complaining. He put his hands on my hips and jerked me towards him. I let out a small moan when I felt his erection rub against me. Were we really doing this? While Asger and Heather were next door?

His tongue swiped across my lip and decided that yes, we were doing this.

He pulled me closer until every inch of my skin was touching him. And still it didn't feel like enough. A strange greed filled me, a desperate need for more. I wrapped my hands around his head, making sure he couldn't escape me. His hair was soft, perfect for tangling my fingers in. His hands were still on my hips, gripping me tight, just as I did to him. It was a strange, passionate kiss, through which both of us showed the other that we weren't going to let them go. Just like he was claiming me, I was claiming him. I wasn't the passive one in this relationship, and I never would be. This was me deciding that I didn't care about convention. I was going to be with all three men, if they would have me. It didn't matter if we called it frille or something else. What mattered was that I'd never have to be without them. Mine. All mine. I was one greedy woman and I didn't care.

The thought of making all three men mine turned me on even more. Kissing the Archivist was no longer enough. I craved them all; wanted them touching me, kissing me, becoming one with me. Would they even agree to that? Sharing me? Maybe I should make it my condition. If they wanted to be with me, they had to share me at least once.

Sandwiched between the two Vikings, the Archivist running his hands over my naked skin...

No, that wasn't just my imagination. He'd actually slipped his hands underneath my shirt. Luckily, he'd given me ordinary clothes, not the restrictive Academy jumpsuit. This made it far easier for him to run his fingers over my back, playing with the clasp of my bra.

It took all my willpower to break the kiss and push him back.

"Not now," I whispered, licking my lips, wishing I hadn't stopped him.

His expression darkened as he watched me move away from him. Not because I didn't want to be near him, but because I had to stop myself from throwing myself at him.

"I see," he said slowly, his voice without any emotion. "I should have known."

"I..."

He didn't let me finish. "Vikings are more exciting, aren't they," he muttered, more to himself than to me, even though his eyes were still focused on my face. "How could a simple Archivist compare to them. I don't have battle scars, no exotic accent, no home in the past. I don't even have a name to offer you." He sighed and smiled sadly. "Go on then. Go to your Vikings and forget this ever happened."

He turned to leave. I was shaking with anger. How dare he think like that?

"Stop," I shouted and he turned, staring at me in surprise. "What the hell are you thinking? Didn't I just kiss you?"

"Yes, but then you stopped." His voice was just a whisper. There was nothing left of the arrogant, gruff Archivist. Was this the man behind the mask? Vulnerable, insecure?

"I said 'not now'," I exclaimed loudly, still almost shouting. Maybe that would get it into his thick skull. "I didn't say 'never'. Right now, in this very moment, we have other things to worry about than how best to get my clothes off. Once we've got Hjalmar back, once this is all settled, then we can continue."

"Continue?" he repeated.

I sighed. "And here I thought that you're clever. I quite liked that kiss and I would like to do it again. There you go. Is that easier to understand?"

"But..."

I gave up. "Not now. Later. Then the three of you can have a chat and decide who of you is going to be the first. Don't make me choose."

"The first?"

Seriously, why did I ever think that he was intelligent? He was turning into a blabbering buffoon.

I pointed at my crotch. "The first. And as much fun as it would be to say that a Viking took my virginity, a 'mysterious man without a name' does have a nice ring to it too." I chuckled. "Although maybe I should make that a condition. That you tell me your name before we go any further."

His eyes widened. "I can't do that."

"Why not? If you want to be with me, there can't be secrets between us. Especially not something as important as your name."

"I-"

Before he could say more, a loud bang made both of us jump. We exchanged a look, then ran back outside to the Archive. Hjalmar was there, standing in the centre of a group of men in black suits. His eyes met mine and the sun seemed to come out from behind thick grey clouds, even though we were underground. He pushed past the men and then I was in his arms, being lifted and pressed to his chest.

I snuggled against him, breathing in his scent.

"I've missed you," he whispered, his voice hoarse.

"I've missed you too." I leaned back a little so that I could look at him. "Are you alright?"

There were lines around his eyes that I was sure hadn't been there before, but the joy in his gaze made up for those.

"Never better now that I've got you in my arms again."

I chuckled. "Cheesy. And romantic."

"I was going for the latter," he muttered with a smirk, but he quickly turned serious. "I was worried about you. Stuck in the past... But I should have known that you can handle yourself."

"Your brother and mother helped."

I realised then that he didn't know about Asger and me. Nor about the Archivist. That was going to be an interesting conversation. For now, though, we had more important things to deal with. Like the men in black surrounding us.

Hjalmar gently lowered me to the floor, his eyes never breaking contact with mine. There was so much emotion in his gaze. So many words that he wanted to say; so many things I wanted to tell him. We'd not known each other for long, but somehow, our separation had made my feelings for him even more intense.

The Archivist cleared his throat.

"Touching," he drawled. He didn't fool me though. I saw through his abrasive demeanour now, no longer deceived by his acting. "Why are you still in my Archive?"

The question was directed at the men in suits.

One of them stepped forward, addressing me. "Madam Priest sends her regards and sees her dealings with you as complete. She trusts you will keep your end of the bargain, or she shall see herself forced to take action."

I sighed. "We've got a contract and I gave her my word. What's done is done, you can leave now."

He gave me a sharp look, then turned to Hjalmar. "I recommend you don't linger for too long."

Hjalmar gave him a nod, but didn't meet my questioning glance. A bad feeling was rising in my stomach. Maybe it had all been too easy. Breaking Hjalmar out of prison at a moment's notice.

The men walked towards the door without another word, but rather than step through it and walk upstairs to the main part of the Academy, they ported, disappearing in a flash of light.

Hjalmar stared at where they'd stood a second ago, then sighed deeply, his shoulders drooping.

"We need to talk."

The Archivist nodded. "Let's go into the room over there. Shall I order us some drinks? Food?"

Hjalmar shook his head. "Better not, we don't want to draw any attention to us. To me, mostly. Although it may be too late for that."

"What's going on?" I asked before we'd even reached the room with the battered leather sofas.

Heather was just as impatient as me. "How did she manage to get you released?"

Hjalmar waited until we were in the room and the door was closed behind us, then wrapped an arm around me and pulled me onto his lap. I leaned against his chest, both happy to have him back and anxious about what was going to happen next.

"A technicality," Hjalmar finally replied. "There are recordings of how they arrested me. They were a little overenthusiastic and used more force than necessary."

I turned on his lap to look at him. "They hurt you?"

Anger was making my cheeks burn. I was going to hurt them in return. Nobody got to touch my Vikings.

He grimaced. I thought it was supposed to be a smile, but it didn't quite reach that level. "Nothing to worry about, but enough for the people in charge to get a little worried. If it's made public how they deal with suspects who've not yet been prosecuted and found guilty, people might not be happy. After all, I'm a teacher at the Academy and usually, we're respected by other agencies, including the enforcers."

"Does that mean they could still come and arrest you again?" Heather asked, voicing my question.

"Aye. I'm free right now because the case could collapse if the video was shown. However, as soon as they get more proof or something else changes, they could come back and put me back in jail." He blinked several times, the only sign how much he hated that thought. "I doubt Mrs Priest would let that happen, but I'm not willing to take the chance."

"She told us she'd get you out of there," I said, my anger still boiling inside my stomach. "Guess I shouldn't have believed her that easily."

"She got me out," he muttered reassuringly. "Even with all her money, she can't work miracles. This is my chance to get away from here and set up a new life before they come for me once more."

Heather had been standing, but now sat down by her son's side and took his hand.

"You know you're always welcome in my home."

Hjalmar smiled at her. "I don't think that's possible. If they somehow manage to track me, I'll put Lucas in danger. No, I need to travel to a new place, a new time. Set up a new life for myself. And I'll have to destroy my bracelet as soon as I get there. I don't want them to be able to pull me back again, or track me. If I disappear, they might simply decide to drop the case, making it easier for them. But if there's even a chance that they could get me back, there are people who will continue to pursue me, no matter how far back in time I go."

The anger inside of me was giving way to fear. Black, cold despair. Hjalmar was going to leave. Lose himself in time. There would be no coming back.

Hjalmar noticed my unease and wrapped his arms around me again, pulling me so close that my chest moved with every breath he took. His beard tickles the nape of my neck. In any other situation, I would have laughed and pushed him away, told him to take his beard off me, but this wasn't the time for joking.

"I can stay," he whispered so low only I could hear. "Without a body to prove that I killed Lucas, I might get ten years at most. If I get a good lawyer and behave well, I might get out soon after you're done with your studies."

I shook my head, glaring at him. "You're not going to prison for something you haven't done. You might act like it's nothing, but I can see you. I can see how you dread the idea. I can see what the two weeks in jail did to you. I won't let you go there again."

I took a deep breath. "I'm coming with you. Wherever you go."

"No."

He stared me down, his expression hardening. "I'm not letting you throw away your life for me. You're young, you've only just started to explore your options. You need to finish your training, make friends, learn what it means to be a time agent. And what about your mother? Are you going to leave her alone?"

His grasp around me loosened, telling me what I was refusing to hear.

He was going to leave me.

Leave me.

Something in me snapped.

ᚠᚼᛒᛁᛏᚢᚱᛁ 22

I was running faster than I'd ever run before. Out of the Archive, up the stairs, along endless empty corridors. I didn't know where I was running until I arrived in front of the door to my room, the dorm I shared with Kaycee. I almost didn't expect the door to open when I pressed my thumb against the fingerprint sensor, but it did.

Kaycee looked up in surprise. She was sitting cross-legged on her bed, watching something on her tablet.

"You," she said, staring at me.

I didn't reply and walked to my part of the room. Except that it wasn't mine anymore. Kaycee's stuff was littered all over my bed, the floor, and I bet the wardrobe no longer contained my own things either. Not that I'd had a lot, but in the two weeks I'd been away, she had acquired a lot of new belongings. Maybe they'd been allowed to go shopping away from the Academy.

Lacking the energy to clear her stuff from my bed, I sank to the floor in front of it. I hugged my legs, the tears I'd held back now threatening to run freely. The shelves in the centre of the room hid me from Kaycee, but the nosy bitch got up and walked around it until she was standing right in front of me.

"Where the hell were you?" she asked, her voice quivering. "Nobody would tell me."

I didn't look up at her. Didn't reply. If I started speaking, I'd choke on my tears.

"I thought you and Hjalmar were dead," she muttered and this time, I looked up in surprise. She actually sounded relieved. I didn't expect that from her.

"Why?" I croaked, just about managing to keep my tears from flowing.

"Both of you just disappeared," she said accusingly. "We were waiting in the classroom and neither of you turned up. First we thought you might have had a quickie in his office, but when Maryam checked, there was no trace of either of you. When you still hadn't turned up by dinner time, we reported it to Sue, who then went to Headmistress Tape. They never told us anything, but their expressions seemed really serious. And then two days later Sue told me that you weren't coming back and that I was going to have the room to myself." She took a deep breath after speaking so quickly. "Are you back for good? Are you going to stay?"

I sighed. "I wish I knew."

And then my eyes betrayed me, and tears began to flow in thick, fast streams.

Kaycee crouched in front of me, but I refused to look at her. It had been a mistake to go back here. I should have found an empty storage room rather than come here where I was running the risk of meeting people I knew. Maryam would have been alright, but this was Kaycee. I couldn't think of a worse person to see me cry.

"Is he dead?" she whispered. "Hjalmar?"

I shook my head.

She sighed in relief. "Thank goodness. They put us in a class on Scottish history instead and I can't stand the teacher. He's not a looker like Hjalmar, and while he talks about kilts all the time, he never bothers to wear one. Not that I'd need to see his knobbly knees."

My tears only increased at her words. She was assuming that he'd come back. That everything would be as before.

It wasn't going to be. Hjalmar would be either in prison or trapped in the past. Either way, he'd be gone. Lost.

I didn't see a way to fix this. If I followed him to the past, what would happen to my mother? The Archivist? Would Asger join his brother or would he want to stay with Heather? There were too many people in this equation. Before I came to TTA, the only person I'd had to think about was my mum. Now, there were so many others. I'd got used to the idea of not seeing my mother for four years while I was at the Academy, but I wasn't prepared to say goodbye to her for good. Besides, me being at the Academy paid for her healthcare. If I wasn't here anymore, I doubted the TTA would continue to pay for her carers. She'd be on her own. Not even Hjalmar could make me do that to her. She was my mother, she'd taken me in when I'd needed a home and I wouldn't abandon her now. Not for a man. Or three.

Slowly, my tears became less. Kaycee handed me a tissue and I stared at her in surprise.

She didn't meet my eyes, as if she was embarrassed to do such a nice gesture. It probably went against her code of being an arrogant bitch.

I blew my nose and wiped my eyes. It was time to be strong. There had to be a way out of this. I was smart, that's why I'd been accepted to the Academy in the first place. I just needed to clear my mind and let my brain think. Ignore my aching heart and think rationally.

"What's going on?" Kaycee asked, becoming slightly impatient. There she was, the Kaycee I knew.

"I can't tell you," I said quickly and got up, swaying slightly as vertigo made my vision flicker. "But I'm going to speak to the Headmistress now."

"Wait, what?"

I ran out of the room before she could ask any more questions.

This was probably a stupid thing to do, and I might regret it, but I didn't know who else to turn to. The head of the Academy had to be clever and know a solution, right?

THE MAN behind the reception gave me a strange look. I realised I wasn't wearing my student uniform, so I probably looked like just a random young woman to him.

"I need to speak to the Headmistress," I said breathlessly. "It's important."

He smiled, his voice patronising. "She is very busy. Do you have an appointment?"

"No, but I need to see her. It's about a teacher."

He raised an eyebrow. "A complaint? We have a form for that."

I sighed impatiently. "No, not a complaint. It's important. I really need to talk to her."

"Trust me, a lot of people want that, but she's a very

busy woman and doesn't have time to speak to random people."

"It's about Hjalmar," I blurted.

He didn't react at all. "Hjalmar?"

I groaned in frustration, trying to remember Hjalmar's full name. He never really used it, probably because Vikings didn't have surnames like we did, names that were passed through generations. They called themselves after their fathers if they were guys, and their mothers if they were women. Heather had mentioned her late husband's name at some point. Think, brain. Think.

Magnus. That would make him... "Hjalmar Magnusson. The teacher. She'll want to see me, trust me."

The man started rummaging on his desk. "There was something about him... ah yes, here it is." He held up a green post-it note. "I'm to..."

A blush spread on his pale cheeks. He pressed a button on his desk and a second later, the holographic image of Headmistress Tape appeared in front of him.

"There's someone here to see you, about Hjalmar Magnusson."

The Headmistress nodded. "Let them in and get us some tea."

"At once, Professor."

I tried hard not to look too triumphant in front of the receptionist, but I couldn't suppress a slight smile when he jumped up and hurried to the door at the other end of the room.

"Keep it brief, she's very busy," he whispered with an annoyed frown before ushering me in.

The Headmistress was sitting behind a large mahogany desk which was bare besides a few small picture frames and a solitary sheet of paper. She signed it with a flourish, then looked up.

"I thought it might be you. Take a seat."

In surprise, I stumbled over my own feet and barely made it to the dark green chair in front of her desk. Luckily, she was inspecting the piece of paper and hopefully didn't me notice me making a fool of myself.

"Is he back?" she asked without preamble.

"Yes, he is," I replied and she smiled at me with true relief. "But I don't know for how much longer."

She put down her pen and leaned back in her high back chair. "Tell me everything."

By the time the receptionist came with a tea tray, I'd filled her in on how we'd managed to get Hjalmar back. I didn't omit anything. It was better that way. The time for secrets was over. I needed help and I wasn't going to get it by sticking to half-truths. I had immense respect for the Headmistress, and hopefully, she would stand up to my expectations.

The man put a mug of tea in front of me. Professor Tape put some milk and sugar in hers, but the receptionist took the tray and left without offering the same to me. I preferred to have sugar in my tea, but that wasn't why I was here.

"I don't know what to do," I admitted as soon as the receptionist had closed the door behind him. "I don't want to be without him, but I also can't leave the Academy."

The Headmistress gave me a sharp look over the rim of her teacup. "While we don't officially forbid relationships between students and teaching staff, we don't tend to support them either. I'm therefore going to ignore what you just said and will focus on how we can keep Hjalmar safe instead."

I swallowed hard, feeling like a little girl being put into her place by a teacher. When filling Professor Tape in on the situation, I'd not omitted telling her about my feelings for him, but I also hadn't mentioned them as such. She was a clever woman though and it was clear that she knew what was going on. Hjalmar wouldn't just have taken a random student into the past, I knew that, and so did she.

"You may think you're the only one who cares about whether he ends up imprisoned or stuck in the past, but you're not. He's one of my most valuable members of staff and I plan to keep it that way, even if he can't stay on as a teacher. I think we're past that point by now." She took a slow, measured sip of tea, while I was fighting hard not to interrupt her.

"I wasn't able to act while he was in jail, but now that he's free, I may have a way to make him untouchable. There's a new scheme being rolled out at the International Centre for Human Rights. Until now, their focus has been on protecting the rights of people living on this Earth in this moment, but time travel is becoming so common that they've decided they need to extend their remit to past times as well. The ICHR is planning to appoint ambassadors for some of the most important historical people and civilisations. Those ambassadors would have diplomatic immunity."

"He'd be untouchable," I whispered, echoing her words.

She nodded with a proud smile. "One of my better

ideas. They'd never appoint someone who's imprisoned, but now that he's free, they will. We need to move fast. I already had a chat with my contacts at the Centre earlier today, but now that you've confirmed his whereabouts, I can get the ball rolling, so to speak."

"What will his role entail?" I asked breathlessly, hope blooming within my chest.

"A lot of time travel," she said, still smiling. "He will have to observe the past, make sure that no Time Agents interfere with events that shouldn't be changed, keep an eye on the treatment of any historic persons extracted from their time for information or other reasons, and many other things. He will be very busy, but he will be based here at the Academy occasionally."

She put down her cup in a very obvious sign that our conversation was at an end. "I will make some calls. Don't leave the Archive, I will send for Hjalmar when everything is sorted."

I nodded and got up. "Thank you, Professor."

There was a lot more I wanted to say, but she was already pulling a tablet from a drawer.

Just when I was about to leave, she cleared her throat. "I'm sure an Ambassador will need an assistant. A work placement for an Academy student, maybe?"

Grinning, I closed the door behind me, ignoring the strange look the receptionist gave me.

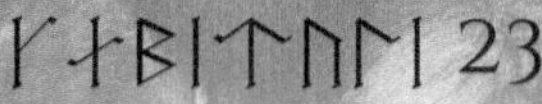

The others were still in the Archive when I returned. As soon as I entered the small room, Heather got up and embraced me in a warm, gentle hug.

"You alright?" she asked.

I nodded, not wanting her to let go. My mother gave hugs like this. I missed her far more than I'd let myself accept. Now that I was in Heather's arms, I realised how much I wanted my mum. She didn't know about Hjalmar yet, nor about the others. She didn't even know that I'd been assigned Vikings as my topic of study. Maybe I could meet her somehow. I'd broken lots of rules already, what would one more count. I hoped she had the care I'd been promised she would get. Carers coming to visit her several times a day, help her with the household, make sure she took her medication. One of the drugs she was taking made her a little forgetful, so it had been one of my jobs to remind her of what she needed to do to stay well.

"The boys have had a chat," Heather whispered, a

smile playing around her lips. "It was rather enlightening."

I instantly stepped back to look at the three men. Asger and Hjalmar were sharing a sofa, and there was no doubt that the two of them were related. Asger's beard was a little wilder and his shoulders were broader from his hard physical work, but their faces were the same. And their expressions. They were hard to read. Was it expectation that they looked at me with? Or something else entirely?

The Archivist was on the sofa opposite, his long legs stretched out in apparent relaxation, but his smile was tense.

Heather took a seat next to him, leaving me standing. I wasn't going to choose who of them to sit with, so I stayed standing, watching them all.

"Good?" Asger asked in his heavily accented voice. I was going to have to give him some English lessons. And improve my own Old Norse. As much as I already felt connected to him, we couldn't be in a relationship without proper communication, and I wasn't going to let Heather or Hjalmar translate for me all the time. There were some things that I wanted to keep private.

I pushed away those thoughts of the future and focused on the present.

"Yes, good." I gave him a tense smile, then turned to Hjalmar. "Professor Tape has a plan that might enable you to stay."

"I can't," he protested, but I didn't let him talk.

"Listen, you big Viking oaf. She's working hard to give you a chance of a normal life, so don't be a martyr before you even know what we might be able to do."

He raised an eyebrow. "We?"

"Well, the Headmistress. She's talking to some Human Rights centre about making you an ambassador for Viking rights. You'd have diplomatic immunity."

"Genius," the Archivist muttered.

"An ambassador?" Hjalmar asked sceptically. "I don't think I'm ambassador material."

Heather chuckled. "You also said that when they made you a teacher, and look at you now. You'd make a great ambassador. You've lived in both worlds, speak both languages, understand the needs of both cultures. You'll be perfect for the role."

"Ambassador?" Asger asked in confusion and Heather quickly spoke to him in Old Norse. I understood the word for people, but that was about it. Studying the language was moving to the very top of my to-do list. As good as I was with reading runes, that wasn't helping me right now, unless the Vikings decided to write me love letters. A love rune stone, now that would be something special. Maybe I could put it in the garden of my future home...

Asger roared in laughter when Heather finished her explanation and slapped his brother on the back. Hjalmar cringed, clearly uncomfortable at the prospect of being in such an important role.

I went over to him and sat on his lap. His arm snaked around my waist, and I wished we were alone. We had some reacquainting to do.

"You'll be great," I reassured him. "And you'll be able to have a normal life. Well, normal for a time travelling Viking."

He snorted. "I might have some sway with my local Viking community, but people here look at me with suspicion now already. How will they react when they find out that I was in prison? Just because I have immunity doesn't mean that the rumours will simply go away. It will undermine my authority before I've even started the job."

"Since when do you care about what other people think?" Heather asked with a cheeky smile. "That's not how I raised you."

"I don't care," he grumbled.

"Let's wait to see what Professor Tape manages to achieve," the Archivist said diplomatically. "And for now, Lainie will be able to continue her studies. With you two gone, I'll keep an eye on her."

He gave me a wink, a promise that he intended to continue what we'd started before. A pleasant shiver ran down my back.

"I stay," Asger growled. "My Lainie."

He reached over and put a hand on my thigh. It was such a possessive gesture that the shiver increased, giving me tingles all over my body.

I wondered what the men had discussed while I'd been gone. They all seemed to be aware of each other's intentions now. How I wished someone had recorded their conversation. Hopefully, Heather would give me a summary later on. I needed to know how they'd reacted to the fact that all three of them were interested in me and that I had no intention to choose.

"I don't think that's a good idea," the Archivist said, his eyebrows arched as he took in Asger. Even though the Viking was wearing clothes that could almost pass as modern, there was something distinctly Norse about him. A raw, untamed energy bubbling beneath the surface. He wasn't going to fit in here, nor would he bother to try. His brother had years of experience in living here, but Asger would stand out like a... well, a Viking in modern society.

"I stay," Asger repeated.

"Maybe we should ask Lainie what she wants?" Heather suggested gently. "Maybe she wants to focus on her studies, and having all of you around would be quite the distraction, I imagine."

I blushed a little. It was strange having the mother of two of my – well, what were they? My boyfriends? That sounded wrong. They weren't boys, they were grown men. My men? My Vikings? My harem of guys? I was going to have to come up with a fitting description.

"Yes, what do you want, sweetie?" the Archivist asked.

I stared at him. "Sweetie? Seriously?"

He shrugged. "That's what they say in films."

"Films?" Asger asked but the Archivist ignored him.

"Should I call you something else instead? Darling? Beautiful?"

I cringed. "Lainie will be fine. This isn't a cheesy romance movie full of blushing girls and sexy men."

"Are we not sexy?" Hjalmar asked, swinging me around in his lap until I was forced to look at him. His eyes were blazing, and heat pooled in my chest, my belly and other parts of my anatomy.

"Ehm..." I stuttered, but luckily, Heather saved me.

"Please don't call my boys sexy in my presence," she chuckled. "There's only so much a mother can take."

"Agreed." I turned around again. "Anyway, the Headmistress is talking to the Human Rights people just now and will send someone down here when she has news. Guess it's us waiting again."

"Seriously though," the Archivist said, not letting go of the topic. "You should stay here. Your training is important and you've already missed two weeks of lessons. Although of course I'd be happy to help you revise."

Once again, he winked. Cheesy. I needed to tell him to stop that. He seemed to get his social skills from films, so no wonder he was so over the top. He'd been holed up down here for far too long. Not that I had any more experience with relationships, but at least I didn't *wink*.

"There might be a slight problem with that," Hjalmar said slowly. "I'm the only Viking Studies teacher at the Academy and I doubt I'd have the time to teach regular classes if I actually become an ambassador. Maybe they'll assign you a different time period. It's only been a couple of weeks so there's still time to start a completely different subject."

I shook my head. "I'm not interested in other subjects. I need to study Old Norse so that I can talk to Asger. It wouldn't make sense for me to be sent to other times when I'm perfectly placed to travel to Viking times where I already know people and have locals to guide me."

"Maybe I could give you some private tuition. You attend general time travel classes here and then you can accompany me for a week or two at a time. Or if my mother could somehow get a time bracer again, she could pick you up here and take you to her place for regular immersions. Asger could teach you and you could teach him."

"She'd get to spend time with all of us," the Archivist

said with a hopeful smile. "Without all of us surrounding her at once."

He said that as if it was a bad thing. Maybe I wanted to be surrounded by them… But he was right. For now, it was better to have them one at a time, and to focus on my studies. I needed to think with my brain, not my ovaries.

"Asger in the past, the Archivist in the present and Hjalmar in both," I summarised.

"I'm in the past too," Heather said with a chuckle.

"Yes. You are. It will be nice to come over for tea," I replied diplomatically.

She laughed again. "Don't worry, you'll get to stay at Asger's house, but I'll be there if you have questions or want some girl time. Also, he's a rubbish cook so if you want proper food, come to my place."

"I cook good," Asger protested, but shut up when his mother raised an eyebrow at him.

"There's one thing though," I muttered, not quite sure how to broach the subject, especially with Heather in the room. "Before we all split up, I'd like to spend some time with all three of you at once. To… ehm… talk things through."

Hjalmar's grip on me tightened. It seemed like he knew what I was alluding to.

"I think that can be arranged," he whispered, his breath hot against my neck.

"My apartment is very secluded," the Archivist offered. It seemed he was trying very hard not to smile.

A bell sounded in the office and he jumped up to see who was interrupting us. I tensed up. What if it was time agents come to arrest Hjalmar again? Or Priscilla Priest's men to silence us after all? I reached out and Asger gripped my hand. If something was about to happen, at least we'd all be in it together.

The Archivist returned to the room a moment later, the Headmistress at his heels. She walked straight to Hjalmar and me and handed him a sealed letter.

A small smile curved her lips.

"Congratulations. Ambassador."

CHAPTER 24

I wasn't sure if the Archivist's bed was going to be big enough for us. It was a double bed, but there were four of us, and the two Vikings weren't exactly small.

Butterflies were whirring in my belly. I'd been so confident about this earlier today, but now that we were actually here, crowded in the Archivists studio flat, I was having second thoughts. I'd never done this before, I had no idea what to do. Maybe I should have practised with one of them before taking on all three. But who? How could I ever make that decision? Hjalmar because I'd met him first? The Archivist because he looked the least like he would squash me? Or Asger because I'd already slept with him in a dream and knew how he felt like?

I focused on that memory, the dream that hadn't been a dream but a memory from the future. I hadn't been a virgin in that one. I'd known exactly what to do. I'd been confident. And I'd loved every second of it. That gave me hope that it wouldn't be so bad. I might be inexperienced but the guys weren't. They could lead me. Right?

"Have you done this before?" I whispered as they stood around me in a circle. The tension between us was almost palpable. None of us moved, but the heat in their eyes made me want to take off my clothes.

Silence followed my question.

Finally, Asger sighed. "No. Wait for you."

Great. One less person who had experience. Although it was incredibly sweet that he had waited for the woman from his dreams. For all he knew, I could have just been a figment of his imagination and he may have waited for nothing.

"Do I look like a lot of girls would throw themselves at me?" the Archivist asked drily.

I turned to him and took him in. Really looked at him. His grey eyes that seemed to swirl with smoke. His fine features, his sharp nose. His glossy dark hair. The tense lines around his lips. Those beautiful lips that had felt so amazing on my own.

"Yes, actually," I croaked, my voice failing me.

He chuckled. "Then you're alone in that. No girls down here, and no girls before I became the Archivist." The smoke in his eyes became more intense when he stepped forward until we almost touched. "Although I have dreamed of you. Of us."

I gaped at him. "Like the dreams Asger had of me?"

"I doubt it," he whispered huskily. "Unless Asger broke into your room at night because he couldn't be apart from you. Unless he climbed in your bed and found you naked beneath your blanket..."

My face was burning. My entire body was trembling

with heat and desire. If just his words could do this, what would his touch do to me?

"Then it was a dream," I whispered, meeting his eyes. "I don't sleep naked."

"Such a pity. Maybe we can change that."

Maybe. Although he didn't seem to be aware that I shared a room with Kaycee. His dreams wouldn't become a reality any time soon, unless my roommate moved out or went on an overnight assignment.

I tore my eyes away from him and turned to Hjalmar. "And you?"

He shrugged. "It seems like I'm going to be the teacher once again. As much as I would like to say that I stayed a virgin for you, I'm not. Although trust me, if I'd known you'd come into my life, I would have stayed celibate."

Fair enough. To be honest, I'd expected all of them to have been with other women. They were older than me, more experienced.

"You're a good teacher," I quipped to get over the tension. "I've learned a lot from you already."

He grinned. "And I'm going to teach you so much more. Starting with how to be undressed by me."

"I can do that myself," I protested, but his hand were already on my shoulders. "Wait. There's one more thing I need to do."

He looked at me in confusion. "If you're worried about protection, I've got some."

I didn't think my face could get any hotter. Especially when I realised that Hjalmar might have to teach Asger about how to use a rubber. Cringe.

"No, I need to have a chat with the Archivist," I hedged. "Give us a moment."

I took his hand before he could say anything and pulled him away, towards the bathroom.

"What's wrong?" he asked when we were out of earshot.

I kept hold of his hand. "I told you before. I want to know your name. I can't be with someone whose name I don't know."

His expression hardened. "I can't do that. Not even for you."

"But why? Why can't you just tell me your name? If it's a really horrible one, I promise I won't make fun of you. I can come up with another one for you. But please, don't let this secret stand between us."

He winced. "I really, really can't. I took an oath."

My eyes widened. "An oath? To keep your name a secret?"

"No, to give it up for good. When I became the Archivist, I gave up my name. I vowed to become the Archivist, to let go of my previous life. It's the only way you can take on this role."

"I don't understand," I whispered. "Why would you have to give up your name for a job?"

He sighed deeply. "This isn't just a job. It's a calling. I can't quit. I can't leave. I'm going to be the Archivist until I die or am too old to keep doing this job. It's the way this Archive works. It becomes your life and you become part of its life."

"This is a room of artefacts, not a living being," I snapped, getting frustrated with him. "I don't get it."

"I should have explained this to you before." He let go of my hand and turned around, lifting the back of his hair. I stood on my tiptoes to see what he was showing me. There was a strange scar at the edge of his hairline.

No, not a scar. A small piece of metal, looking like a part of electronics."

"What is that?" I asked, not able to suppress a gasp.

"My connection to the Archive. The information stored in this place is too vast, too valuable to keep on a normal server. Computers can't make the intricate connections between an item and its previous owner. The rules of what item to give to what time traveller. They need a human mind. When you become the Archivist, you accept the Archive not just into your life, but into your mind."

I was having trouble following him. I'd never come across anything like it.

"Does that mean you're a cyborg?" I asked after a while of staring at the scar.

He laughed and turned around again. His eyes were twinkling with mirth.

"No, I'm still as human as you. I'm not enhanced in any way... not that I'd need to be." He winked again. I really needed to tell him not to do that, as cute as it was. "But you need to understand that I can't give up the Archive. Not even for you."

"What does that mean though? Do you have to stay here forever? Can you go on holidays? Retire early? Do they even pay you?"

Again, he laughed. "Yes, they pay me, although I've never had much of a reason to spend my money. I get this flat and as much food as I want as part of my job, and it's not like my clothes get worn out quickly down here so I rarely have to go shopping. But yes, I can go on holidays. Usually, I combine a research trip for work with a couple of days off. I get to travel in time a lot, to source new artefacts or to try out existing ones, and I like to take a few days to explore and meet the locals."

"And visit family?"

A shadow passed over his expression. "No family. One of the reasons I became the Archivist. There's nobody who would miss me. Nobody who would hold on to the old me."

"Well, I'm going to hold on to the new you, the current you," I promised, and his smile returned. "But I really want to give you a proper name. I can't call you the Archivist forever. That's just weird."

He shrugged. "I don't think there's a rule that prevents anyone from calling me whatever they want, as long as I stay the Archivist at the same time."

"I shall come up with something good. Something pretty."

"If you have to. But I have veto rights."

I grinned. "Done. I'll try and find a name that's universal, one that works across different times. Like James."

He pouted. "Not something as boring as that."

"Don't worry, I'll come up with something extraordinary. For now, how about Archie?"

He shuddered. "Don't you dare."

CHAPTER 25

Two naked Vikings were expecting us, lying next to each other in the Archivist's bed. There wasn't going to be any space for the rest of us. I tried to keep my eyes focused on their faces, but I couldn't resist a quick peek. They were almost the same size, but Asger was hairier. I'd seen him naked before, in our dream, and when I'd talked to him right after we'd shared that dream, but it was different to see him in the flesh. There was a lot of flesh. How did he manage to be so broad without being fat?

When I'd been in the shed with Hjalmar, it had been dark and I had been far too out of it to take much note of his looks. Now, I regretted that. He was gorgeous. Those toned thighs, his defined abs, ... He was perfect.

I'd only ever seen men naked on tv, so I'd always thought that once I'd finally be with one for real, I'd be severely disappointed. The opposite was true. They were so much better than all those pretty boys. These were men.

Hjalmar lazily smiled up at me. "I thought by now you'd have got rid of those clothes."

What did he think the Archivist and I had got up to?

"Archivist, take off her shirt."

A shiver ran through me at his husky words. Hjalmar was giving orders now. Was he going to direct us all, set the scene, guide us?

The Archivist gave me a questioning look and I nodded. My knees were starting to wobble, and I was glad that he was standing right behind me, ready to catch me if I suddenly collapsed. Not that I was planning to do that, but my body was feeling stranger than it ever had before. Everything was so much more intense. My heartbeat pulsed through my veins, bringing heat to my core. Seeing the two Vikings naked in front of me made me wet and ready for them.

"Arms up," the Archivist whispered. I did as he said, stretching my arms into the air. He pulled my shirt up and over my head, leaving me in just my bra. The Archivist had given it to me earlier, but it was a little too small and my boobs were spilling over the top.

He gently put his warm hands on my breasts, rubbing against the bra. I wish he would take it off, but instead, he started massaging my boobs through the silky material. My nipples were hard, aching to be freed and touched.

"Take it off," Hjalmar commanded to my relief.

I actually sighed when the Archivist slid my bra down my arms and let it fall to the floor.

For a moment, I felt a little exposed. Here I was, half-naked, with three men staring at me as if I was a delicious meal. But then, I bet that was exactly how I was looking at the Vikings. And how I would look at the Archivist once he was naked and on the bed.

Without waiting for more instructions from Hjalmar, the Archivist put his hands on my breasts again. His skin was soft and warm, and his touch just the right balance between too little and too much. He spread his fingers and took my nipples between them, rubbing against them back and forth.

I moaned. My breasts had always been sensitive, and when I made myself come, I always kept one hand on them, squeezing as I brought myself to my climax. Having someone else do it was an entirely different feeling though.

I leaned back, pressing against the Archivist's hard chest. If he continued like this, I'd be a writhing mess on the floor, unable to keep upright.

"Take off the rest of her clothes," Hjalmar ordered. I moaned in protest when the Archivist took his amazing hands off my breasts. My nipples were sore, aching to be touched, to be worshipped.

"Soon," Asger chuckled. He was watching me intently, one hand stroking his erection. He was hard, ready, waiting. And big. I'd easily taken him in my dream, but I'd probably slept with him many times before then, I'd been used to his size. Now, I wasn't. I swallowed at the thought of somehow fitting him inside me. But if women managed to press children out of there, his cock had to fit.

I'd not seen the Archivist's shaft yet, but if he was smaller, he was going to be the first. To ease me in gently. I could feel his hardness pressing against my back. He was the only one still fully dressed. Hopefully, that would change soon.

"Stop thinking," Hjalmar told me, as if he knew that I was having a hard time bringing my thoughts in order.

"Just relax. Go with the flow. We'll be gentle with you, don't worry. We'll go slow."

I nodded and relaxed against the Archivist's hold. He had an arm wrapped around my waist to hold me steady, while he was trying to open my jeans with one hand. When he continued to fumble, I reached down and helped him open the button and pull down the zip. I knew my panties were showing now. The last part of clothing shielding me from their eyes. This was the point of no return.

I took a deep breath and pulled down my jeans along with my panties, stepping out of them and my shoes as fast as I could. Now I really was naked.

The Archivist was still pressed against me, the fabric of his clothes reminding me with every touch that he was still dressed.

"Close your eyes," Hjalmar said softly. "Let him hold you."

With one last look at the two men, both of them stroking their hard cocks, desire sparkling in their eyes, I did as he'd said. I leaned into the Archivist's body.

His breath was going fast, brushing against the nape of my neck, tickling me. His erection was hard, large, pressing into my back. I kind of wished I could turn and help him with that, but I knew Hjalmar had a plan for how this was going to play out.

The Archivist's hands roamed my body, sliding over my stomach, my chest, my thighs, avoiding the places I really wanted him to touch. When his fingers finally reached the triangle between my legs, I sighed deeply.

Slowly, he cupped my mound, then started flicking my clit with his thumb. For someone who'd never done this before, he knew exactly how to touch me. This wasn't hapless fumbling, this was a maestro playing his instrument.

When he slid a finger between my folds, I moaned loudly. Shivers ran up and down my body, and my skin seemed to be burning with a strange heat that needed an outlet.

"More," I whispered huskily, but he didn't follow my wishes. He kept his finger inside me, but didn't move, didn't do anything, didn't even rub my clit. I groaned in frustration.

"Give her another one," Hjalmar ordered and I could have kissed him in gratitude.

Slowly, a second finger joined the first, stretching me. I could take it, I'd done this before myself, but his fingers were larger than mine and I did notice the difference. When he was fully inside me, he started rubbing my clit again, eliciting rows of tiny moans that tumbled from my lips.

"I love the sounds you make," he whispered into my ear. "Don't stop."

I wouldn't have been able to. I was too far gone already, bound to react to his every touch.

"Another," Hjalmar said. His dominant voice totally turned me on. I wondered if he was still staring at me full of lust and desire, but I didn't dare open my eyes.

This time, it hurt a little when the Archivist pushed a third finger into me. He was slow and gentle, letting me adjust, while distracting me with his other hand taking hold of my breast. Just what I had needed. Pressure was building inside of me, the combined power of all the touches he was giving me. I was close already. If this continued, I'd come before any of them even entered me.

"Spread your legs a little," Hjalmar demanded, and I

immediately did as he said. It made the fullness a little more bearable. More pleasant. I had the urge to push forward my hips, moving against the Archivist's hand, but I just about managed to refrain.

"Does that feel good?" Hjalmar asked.

All I could do was nod and moan. I was no longer capable of forming words.

"Carry her to the bed. It's time. Lainie, keep your eyes closed."

I moaned in disappointment when the Archivist's fingers slipped out of me. I was empty, too empty. I needed him back. I groaned and turned in his arms, but he held me tight and lifted me up. I clung to his grip until he gently put me down on the bed. Warmth came from both sides. I was lying in between the two brothers. The naked Vikings who were going to make me happy. That thought alone was enough to bring me to the edge.

The sound of a zipper announced that the Archivist was following suit and getting naked like the rest of us.

"Do you want to know who's first?" Hjalmar whispered from my right. "Or do you want it to be a secret?"

"Secret," I moaned, surprised at what he was doing. "But I know where you all are."

Hjalmar chuckled. "Not for much longer. "Archivist, do you have a scarf?"

By the time I had figured out what they were doing, a scarf was wrapped around my eyes. I relaxed a little, no longer having to fight to keep my eyes closed. The temptation to peek was gone.

Hjalmar said something in Old Norse and he and his brother got off the bed, leaving me alone.

"No," I muttered. "Don't leave me."

"We're never going to leave you," the Archivist promised. "Paper, scissors, stone?"

That question had to be directed to the other men. Hjalmar whispered some more in Old Norse, then there was only silence.

A movement in the air warned me moments before someone touched my thighs. I tried to feel if his palms were callused, if it was Asger, but before I could focus my senses enough, something pressed against my entrance.

There were no more orders from Hjalmar. No more whispered encouragements from the Archivist. I felt them all close to me, but they didn't reveal who they were.

Hands cupped my breasts, lips kissed my belly, while a cock was still there, at my very core, ready to push in.

When lips closed around my nipple, I moaned, and that seemed the signal for them to begin.

The pressure increased and the cock's tip penetrated my folds, pushing in slowly but surely. I opened my thighs further, making it easier for him. The stretching became painful, my moan turning into a slight cry, but then he pushed in and it was done. He was inside me. One with me.

He stayed like that for a bit, while the others still touched my body, their tongues and fingers leaving traces of fire across my skin. Neither of them tried to kiss me, probably aware that I would be able to tell who they were. They each had a different taste, a unique scent that put them apart.

As if he could sense that I was adjusting to his girth, the man inside me slowly pulled back, but then pushed in again before he was fully out. His thrusts were slow, careful, but intense enough for me to unravel. When he pushed in again and his thumb rubbed against my clit, I cried out, no longer able to hold back. I came, crashing against him, riding the wave of ecstasy that their touches were creating. They didn't stop, made me moan and moan, made me quiver, shake on the mattress, squirm beneath them. One cock gave way to another, then another, until they'd all merged with me. I was floating, kind of regretting that I didn't have the energy to return their kisses, their touches, but I was busy trying not to black out.

Just when I thought it was over, someone kissed my core, slowly licking away the slight tinge of pain that was still lingering there, and I came apart once more, shaking in their arms, listening to their whispered words of love.

EPILOGUE

ONE MONTH LATER

I blinked up at the sun. Strange how it looked exactly the same no matter in what time I was. I closed my eyes and let the warmth seep through my skin. It was a cold morning and I missed central heating, but I should be grateful that Asger had been stirring the fire throughout the night, making sure that it was still on when we got up.

He was humming to himself in the smithy behind the house. I smiled. He was adorable sometimes, especially when he didn't think anyone was watching. Or listening, in this case. He was slightly out of tune, or maybe it was supposed to be that way. I hadn't come across Norse music yet, but Asger planned to introduce me to some of his friends tonight.

"Beautiful morning."

Hjalmar stepped out of the door behind me, a towel wrapped around his waist, his chest bare. I turned and let him press a soft kiss on my lips.

"It really is. It's so quiet here."

He chuckled. "Sometimes I think it's too quiet, but after the last few weeks, I'm grateful for it. We needed this break."

I wrapped an arm around him and closed my eyes again. I felt grounded here, more at home than I would ever feel at the Academy. I almost wished I could stay in this village, live their uncomplicated lives, but at the same time, I loved studying. Having been here, having realised how little I knew, had given me the urge to learn as much as possible. Every night, I went through my vocabulary lists before going to bed, hoping that the words would somehow take root while I slept. Unless I sneaked down into the Archive and spent the night there. Kaycee hadn't commented on it yet, but I was sure she would soon. For now, she was strangely quiet, as if she was too shy to ask all the questions she had to have. I liked her that way. I guessed we'd all changed since we arrived at the Academy.

Something tickled my nose. A smoky smell that didn't come from the smithy.

Hjalmar groaned. "I think he's burning the eggs again! Why do we let him make breakfast?"

I laughed as he ran back into the house, looking ready to kill the Archivist.

This was the first time all four of us were together again since the day Hjalmar had been named Ambassador. It had been a whirlwind of lessons, studying and stolen kisses in between. While I got to see the Archivist every day, Hjalmar had only managed to visit me twice, and Asger had been back here with his mother the entire time. Well, it had only been three days for him, we'd made sure to time our arrival in the best possible way. I'd been without him for a month, yet he'd not had to wait as long. I almost envied him, but then, it had given me the chance to spend more time with the Archivist.

We still hadn't decided on a name. It was hard, and getting harder with each day. In my mind, he was the Archivist, with a capital A, and turning him from that into an ordinary name seemed impossible. He wasn't ordinary, not in the slightest. I'd come to realise how much the Archive really was a part of him. It gave him a unique way of looking at the world, seeing history in a different way. Sadly, it didn't teach him how to make breakfast.

I smiled and wrapped my woollen shawl closer around my body. Even though the morning was cold, it looked like it was going to be a beautiful day. I wasn't sure yet what we were going to do, but it probably involved eating lots of food, relaxing in the sunshine and meeting other Vikings.

I was looking forward to that. Last night, Asger had taught me some fun curses and I was itching to try them out on someone. He'd told me some terms of endearment too, but I wasn't going to use them on anyone but my men. Tonight though... I was going to make Hjalmar proud. He was still my teacher, after all. Headmistress Tape had managed to convince the Human Rights Centre to let him teach Viking Studies once a month for three days at a time. Since Kaycee and Maryam had changed to other courses though, these three days were time I got to spend with him. His teaching came in many shapes and forms, and he definitely taught me a lot. At a desk, on a desk and on the floor next to a desk. I was coming to understand that Vikings were talented in a lot of ways. While the Archivist and I were exploring what was possible together, when I was with Hjalmar, he took charge.

My smile widened and I blinked at the sun once more. It was such a beautiful day. I had three amazing men in the house behind me, all of them eager to spend time with me.

I had to be the luckiest person alive; now, in the future and in the past.

ENDIR

*This concludes Lainie's story, although read on for a **bonus scene** from the guys' POV.*

While I might return to her and her men in the future, each of the other Academy of Time books focus on new people and a new time period - although some of the characters will be familiar.

Want to travel to medieval Scotland and meet Mary Queen of Scots? Read Saving His Queen.

How about a trip to the Great Library of Alexandria? Enter Exploring Her Professor and solve an ancient mystery.

To find out about all my books and new releases, subscribe to my newsletter: skyemackinnon.com/newsletter

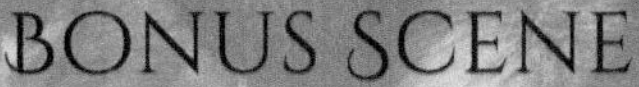

BONUS SCENE

"The boys have had a chat," Heather whispered, *a smile playing around her lips. "It was rather enlightening."*

But what actually did they discuss while Lainie was talking to the headmistress?

Let's be a fly on the wall...

HJALMAR

I want to run after her, but my brother grasps my wrist.

"Don't. Give her some time. She's been through a lot recently."

For the first time since I've returned, I properly look at him, then smile. I've missed my brother. We clasp arms, but I can't help but wince when his thumb presses against one of my many bruises. I'll never tell Lainie what happened to me in prison, but despite the bravado I showed, the fake bravery that made her leave, despite that, I don't want to go back there. My entire body hurts, and even though most of my wounds are healing already, each bruise is a reminder of what I went through.

Asger glances down at my arms and raises a knowing eyebrow. He was once a prisoner of war, but I managed to fight our way into their village and get him back. I bet he would have done the same for me, but in this world, problems aren't resolved with swords and axes. Here, money does the talking. Money and power, and I have neither.

"I need to tell you something," Asger says, meeting my eyes. It's like looking into a mirror, except that his beard is wilder than mine. "There are things you need to know."

I give him a court nod and motion towards the sofas. "Let's sit down."

My mother is sitting opposite us, the Archivist by her side. He smiles, but his expression is tense, like there are things he wants to say as well. A lot seems to have happened while I was gone.

"Mother, can you translate for the futureman?" Asger asks. I smirk at his choice of words. There are no archives in the past, no libraries. There is no word to translate the Archivist's title, and I don't know his name, nobody does. It's part of his role, I believe. He gives up his name when he takes the position. I've never quite understood why, but it's tradition.

"Of course," mother says with a smile. "Just don't make it too explicit. I don't need to hear the details."

I stare at her. Explicit? A knot is forming in my stomach.

Asger takes a deep breath. "Do you remember the dreams I had? The ones about the woman?"

I nod, dreading where this might go. "Had? Have they stopped?"

He smiles sheepishly. "They have, ever since I met the woman from my dream. She's real, Hjal. She's actually real."

The knot is getting bigger. "Please don't tell me-"

"It's her," he blurts out. "It's Lainie. We are linked, bound to each other. She feels the same, I still can't believe it. All these years... The dreams were real. Prophecy. And then she had the same dream, and she knew about... well, my little disability." He cringes and his hand grabs his crotch. He probably doesn't even realise he's doing it. "It's destiny, Hjal. True destiny. Lainie and I are made to be with each other."

Dread fills me. He's so convinced of it, and if Lainie feels the same... Have I lost her? I've only been gone for a couple of weeks, was that enough for me to lose her? I didn't think she'd do that. I had her down as someone loyal, but it seems I was mistaken.

I get up, shrugging off my brother's hand. "I see."

"Sit back down," my mother says softly. "Let him finish."

I don't want to, I want to run and hit something, but the quiet authority in her voice makes me take a seat again. This time, I'm leaving some space between Asger and me.

"She loves you," Asger says without warning. I look at him in surprise.

"Didn't you just say that she wants to be with you?"

I don't think I've ever felt that many confusing emotions at once. I pride myself on my self-control, but this is too much. I ball my hands into fists, fighting the urge to storm out of the room.

"Frille."

That one, simple word makes the knot in me shudder and unravel.

"Frille is for men," I mutter weakly, but my mind is racing. Could it be? Could she really want several men? Both of us. Asger and me.

"She's not bound by our laws and traditions. I told her about frille to make her understand that she doesn't have to choose. She was so worried about what to do, but I think she's come to understand that she isn't forced to make a choice." He pauses for a moment. "If you're alright to share."

THE ARCHIVIST

I'm not sure if Heather is translating everything the two Vikings are saying. They seem to be exchanging a lot more words than she is passing on. I hope she's not mincing their words; I need to know what's going on. I speak many languages, but Old Norse isn't one of them, and I feel helpless to be relying on her to do the translating. It must be strange for her, listening to them talk about a girl both of them fancy.

"Hjalmar says he's prepared to share," Heather informs me.

I didn't expect that. Hjalmar is a dominant, powerful man and I'd doubted he'd give up his claim on Lainie for anyone, not even his brother. Now the question is whether that willingness to share also extends to me.

I clear my throat and both Norsemen turn to me.

"I want her too," I tell them without preamble. This

isn't the time to beat around the bush. Their eyes widen at the same time. Heather doesn't need to translate this, Asger seems to understand.

"Want Lainie?" he asks in his heavily accented voice.

I nod, meeting his eyes defiantly. "We kissed. She said she wants all three of us."

This time, he waits until Heather translates it. A smile plays around her lips as she does so. She seems to be enjoying this. For someone who's lived in the past for decades, she's very progressive and accepting.

I would tell them that she even talked about one of us taking her virginity, but I don't want to do that in front of Heather. She's their mother, after all, and she doesn't need to hear all the details. Maybe later, when we're alone, and Hjalmar can translate for his brother. If this is indeed turning into one big relationship, Asger will have to learn more English.

"Did she actually say that?" Hjalmar questions, a frown appearing above his thick eyebrows. "In those words?"

I sigh. "She said she wanted to kiss me again, and that she also wants to be with the two of you. Unless she simply likes kissing random people, I'd interpret that as her wanting to be with all three of us."

"That's going to be so complicated," Hjalmar mutters. "Relationships are difficult enough when it's just two people."

I couldn't agree more. Not that I have any experience with relationships. I've been holed up in this place for most of my life, and I never had a girlfriend before I took this role. Besides one entirely fling with an assistant teacher a couple of years ago – just to see what all the fuss was about, really, although we never got past kissing - I've been single and fairly happy with that. Now, that's all going to change. When Lainie crashed into me on that corridor, she didn't just crash into my body. She crashed into my heart.

Asger

Three of us. The futureman wants her too. I shouldn't be surprised, Lainie is the most beautiful woman I've ever seen. Not just on the outside, but on the inside too. She's got a light to her, a strong flame flickering within her, that seems to attract us like insects. For her, I'll gladly be a fly. I'll be small and insignificant as long as I can have her.

I *know* her. I may not have exchanged a lot of words with her, but my dreams have shown me all about her. I know her desires, her fears, her dreams. I'm going to make her dreams come true and her fears disappear. I'm going to protect her from pain and loss, and if that means I have to die for her, so be it. I'm going to be her warrior. I'm going to take up my sword again, put my smithy hammer away, and be her guardian. Nobody will ever hurt her. And I will go after the people who hurt her in the past. I've not seen the details in her dreams, but I've felt her fear. Something happened to her and I'm going to find out what. And then I'm going to kill them.

Hjalmar and the futureman are talking in English, but I don't try to comprehend. All I want to do is imagine Lainie in my arms. She will be there a lot. I won't let her go easily. Yes, I might be prepared to share, but when it's my turn, I will have her and hold her and treasure her.

Lainie is mine. And theirs. We are her frille and we're going to look after her.

Enjoyed this? Want more reverse harem? I've put the first books in three different series into one starter box set, Daggers and Destiny, so you can decide which series you feel like reading next.

OLD NORSE VOCABULARY

Here are some handy Old Norse phrases, just in case you get to meet your own sexy Viking(s).

First of all, this is just a basic list that doesn't cover all the declinations needed to differentiate between addressing a man, woman, or group of people.

For example, a simple 'hello' would have to be declined in the following five ways:

Heill! - to greet one man
Heil! - to greet one woman
Heilir! - to greet a group of men
Heilar! - to greet a group of women
Heil! - to greet a group including both sexes

Since doing that for every word would make this book twice as long, take these phrases with the knowledge that you may not be using perfect grammar – but I'm sure your Norseman will be happy to correct you.

Ek ann þér – I love you (lit. I grant you [love]) - ᛁᚴ ᛆᚿ ᚦᛁᛦ
Já – Yes
Nei - No
Hei - Hi (informal greeting)
Góðan dag/Góðan daginn - Good day
Góðan morgin - Good morning
Góðan aptan - Good afternoon
Gott kveld - Good evening
Sofðu vel - Good night (sleep well)
Allt er gott - That's okay
Hvaðan ertu? – Where are you from?
Ek em frá ... - I am from ...
Ek em einhleypr ♂ / mey ♀ – I am single
Gørðu svá vel - Please
Dey! - Die!
Hvar er hjálmr minn? - Where is my helmet?
Fífl! - Fool!
Hel taki þik! - May Hel take you!
Far þú í arsgat! - Fuck off! (lit. Go into the arsehole!)
Hrafnarnir munu hafa þik! - The ravens will have you!

NOT-SO-FUN FACT

The scene where Asger and the people from his village are almost burned to death by their enemies is inspired by real events, such as the 'Burning in Upsal'.

King Ingjald, Onund's son, came to Gamla Uppsala in Sweden (near the city of Uppsala), the residence of Swedish kings. He built a great hall with seven thrones and invited all the important kings and jarls. Six kings came, and when they were drunk, Ingjald and his men left the hall, barred the doors and set it on fire, killing anyone who tried to escape. Ingjald then took possession of the dead kings' territories. In a twist of karma, he later died himself by being burned in his own hall.

Red Wedding, anyone?

(Although that one is inspired by events at Edinburgh Castle in 1440, but that's another story.)

"Konung Ingjald Illråda bränner upp 6 Fylkiskonungar" by Hugo Hamilton (1802–1871). 1830. Teckningar ur Skandinaviens Äldre Historia. Stockholm: Gjöthström & Magnusson. Digitalized by Martling Bok & Grafik.

RESOURCES

As mentioned in the introduction, here are some resources that I found particularly helpful while studying Old Norse and Runology. This is by no means an extensive list and I'm sure there are some great other resources out there that I've not come across yet (if you know something good, email me!).

My favourite book: '*Viking Language 1: Learn Old Norse, Runes, and Icelandic Sagas*' by Jesse Byock. ISBN 978-0988176416

A free Memrise course teaching the most important 246 Old Norse words mentioned in the book:
https://www.memrise.com/course/365561/the-246-top-old-norse-words-audio/

Some short videos about Norse culture and studies:
http://www.vikingnorse.com/old-norse-teaching-videos

English to Old Norse Dictionary:

http://www.
vikingsofbjornstad.com/Old_Norse_Dictionary_E2N.sht
m

The Futhark song (like the ABC song but for the Futhark):
http://www.sassafrassmusic.com/songs/norse-
mythology/futhark-song/

Dr Jackson Crawford's Old Norse YouTube channel (lots
of fun stuff):
https://www.youtube.com/channel/UCXCxNFxw6iq-
Mh4uIjYvufg/featured

The Orkneyinga Saga in English translation:
https://archive.org/details/
orkneyingasaga00goudgoog/page/n12

More information about runes:
https://www.omniglot.com/writing/runic.htm

All sorts of interesting Viking facts:
https://www.vikingrune.com/

Including a fascinating article on Viking hairstyles:
https://www.vikingrune.com/2014/03/viking-hairstyles-
is-ragnars-haircut-historical/

Love and Marriage in Viking times:
http://avaldsnes.info/en/viking/kjaerlighet-og-ekteskap/

Elder Futhark

ACADEMY OF TIME

A series of standalones set in the same world, full of action, intrigue and steamy romance, set in both past and present. Some are reverse harem, some are m/f.

Taking Her Vikings

A full-length steamy reverse harem full of action, intrigue and hot Vikings, set in both past and present. Includes resources to learn basic runes and Old Norse!

Exploring Her Professor

An m/f romance full of mystery and riddles set in Ancient Egypt.

Saving His Queen

An m/f romance about the tragic life of Mary, Queen of Scots.

About the Author

Skye MacKinnon is a USA Today & International Bestselling Author whose books are filled with strong heroines who don't have to choose.

She embraces her Scottishness with fantastical Scottish settings and a dash of mythology, no matter if she's writing about aliens in kilts, Celtic gods, cat shifters, or the streets of Edinburgh.

When she's not typing away at her favourite cafe, Skye loves dried mango, as much exotic tea as she can squeeze into her cupboards, and being covered in pet hair by her demon cat Sootie.

Subscribe to her newsletter:
skyemackinnon.com/newsletter

Join her Facebook group:
facebook.com/groups/skyesbookharem

www.ingramcontent.com/pod-product-compliance
Lightning Source LLC
Chambersburg PA
CBHW030746190726
48285CB00003B/717